PRINCE WILLIAM, Maximilian Minsky and Me

Holly-Jane Rahlens was born in Queens, New York, and now lives in Berlin with her husband and son. She moved to Germany after graduating from Queens College but remains an American citizen and a frequent visitor to the United States. Written in English, *Prince William, Maximilian Minsky and Me* was translated into German and earned the prestigious Deutscher Jugendliteraturpreis as the best young adult novel published in Germany. She says, "I wrote this book to remind myself and all my readers that life is not simply black and white. In other words, the smartest girl in the class can actually be the dumbest. An *enfant terrible* can turn out to be Prince Charming. We can put our faith in the laws of science yet still embrace our religious roots. And even a city with a dark past like Berlin can, indeed, become a haven of light."

PRINCE WILLIAM, Maximilian Minsky and Me

HOLLY-JANE RAHLENS

WALKER
BOOKS

This is a work of fiction. Names, characters, places, and
incidents are either products of the author's imagination or,
if real, are used fictitiously.

First published in Great Britain 2007 by Walker Books Ltd
87 Vauxhall Walk, London SE11 5HJ

2 4 6 8 10 9 7 5 3 1

Copyright © 2002 Rowohlt Taschenbuch Verlag GmbH,
Reinbek bei Hamburg
English language text © 2005 Holly-Jane Rahlens
Published by arrangement with Rowohlt Verlag GmbH

The right of Holly-Jane Rahlens to be identified as author
of this work has been asserted by her in accordance
with the Copyright, Designs and Patents Act 1988

This book has been typeset in Sabon

Printed and bound in Great Britain by
Creative Print and Design (Wales), Ebbw Vale

British Library Cataloguing in Publication Data:
a catalogue record for this book is available
from the British Library

ISBN 978-1-4063-0547-0

www.walkerbooks.co.uk

As always,
for Noah and Eberhard,
my two and only

Nerd Nelly

Once upon a time, in a far and distant land—well, okay, to be exact, it was just a couple of years ago and right here in Berlin—I discovered the future king of Great Britain, William Arthur Philip Louis Windsor, also known as Wills, better known as Prince William, son of His Royal Highness the Princeof Wales, Charles Philip Arthur George Mountbatten Windsor, and his ex-wife, Diana, Princess of Wales, formerly known as Lady Diana Frances Spencer, no longer among us. It was love at first sight. It changed my life completely.

But before I get into all the details, let me tell you a little about myself. Everyone knows who Prince William is, right? But who in the world is Nelly Sue Edelmeister?

When Prince William came into my life, I was an incredibly intense thirteen-year-old, a skinny Berlin schoolgirl with a fat braid down my back, thick glasses plastered across my face, and a brain the size of the *Encyclopaedia Britannica*. I was a mess. In America, where my mother grew up, they call kids like me "nerds." And that's exactly what I was: an overachieving jerk. I mean, I was the type who walked down the street with her nose stuck in a book *all* the time. Usually you only see people walking down the street with their noses stuck in books in the movies. You don't come across them that much in real life because it actually requires a great deal of skill to maneuver safely down the street without looking, especially in a city like Berlin, where any second you could be attacked by a rabid Rottweiler if you don't watch out, or, even worse, accidentally step in its poop. But read and walk I did. And when I got home, I simply cleaned off my shoes — if I remembered, that is.

"It's like the Middle Ages!" my mother would say when she saw me scraping away the ick from her good Persian carpet. "For people as organized as the Germans, in a city as anal as Berlin, where in every damn courtyard they separate their garbage into a dozen different categories — paper, cardboard, plastic, organic trash, green glass, brown glass, clear glass, *magenta* glass, for all I know! My God, you would think they would know how to clean up after their dogs! They wouldn't stand for crap like this in New York!"

My mother, Lucy Bloom-Edelmeister, never stopped comparing Berlin to her hometown. And you could always hear the exclamation point at the end of her sentences. "I left New York," she'd say, "but it never left me!" After a visit to Berlin in the early eighties, she found so much to dislike about the city, she decided to stay and make an art out of complaining about it. She met my father about ten boyfriends and one year later. Papa's a musician, a clarinetist known as Bazooka Benny, although his real name is Bernhard Nicholas Edelmeister. He and my mother met while switching trains in the subway at Möckernbrücke, at the middle-level frankfurter stand. They fell in love over a currywurst, moved in together, and the rest is history. They lived with a couple of friends in Schöneberg, in the apartment where rock star David Bowie once lived—or so they say—but when my mother was pregnant with me, they took over the place here in Wilmersdorf, where we've been ever since.

Wilmersdorf's on the west side of town. Some parts of it are posh. But a lot is just plain old hum-drum. A bit is a little rundown. Our building is absolutely dilapidated. The plaster on the façade is crumbling all over the place, and you can see the brick and mortar peeking out from underneath. My parents agree that our building looks as bad as the worst houses in the east. (It's practically the *only* thing they agree on, but more about that later.) As long as I can remember, the basement in our house has always smelled of mildew and mold, and whenever I go down there, I can see mice scurrying to get out of our way. My mother says they're rats, not mice, but then my father says to her, "How do you know? When was the last time you were down there? Ten years ago?"

The landlord, Herr Pomplun, who lives next door to us with three German shepherds and an urn full of his dead wife's ashes, refuses to renovate the house. Every once in a while my mother threatens Pomplun by saying she's going to report him to the authorities. And maybe she will. "She's one tough cookie," my father's always saying. "Made in USA. One hundred percent chutzpah." But mostly my mother just shrugs and says, "Thank God it's the people across the street who have to look at the house, not me."

My mother's ex-best friend, Beate, who plays Nurse Bettina in the German television soap opera *University Clinic,* lives across the street. She and my mother met years ago when my mom interviewed her for a magazine. Beate has a duplex with something like fifteen rooms, just as many bathrooms, and a roof garden. "It's buildings like that that make the neighborhood nice," my mother used to say. But these days she says, "It's pompous buildings like that that raise the rent sky-high around here."

Anyway, as I said, when I was thirteen, I was a nerd who liked to read a lot. I read everything. But mostly I was into the sciences. I was preparing myself for a career in astronomy or cosmology and was forever gathering information about super strings, baby universes, black holes, time warps—you get the picture.

I got into astronomy the summer I was nine. My parents sent me off to New York to stay with my mother's brother, my uncle Bruce, and his wife, my aunt Debbie. They lived in Manhattan, on the Upper West Side, in a tiny little two-bedroom apartment. The day their air conditioner broke down and I almost died of heat stroke, they stuck me into this young people's astronomy program at the Hayden Planetarium, just a short walk from their house. It cooled me off and blew my mind. I adored sitting under the planetarium's air-conditioned night sky on an unbearably sweaty and sunny afternoon, contemplating the cosmos. I decided then that it would be my life's goal to solve the mysteries of the universe.

Anyway, the summer I turned thirteen, I was a book buff and I was star-struck. And I was also into my computer. In fact, that's where I first got to really know and appreciate Prince William: on the Internet, studying the queen's homepage and the websites dedicated to the royals. When my mother discovered my secret, the first thing she said was, "Ah, love at first site."

Ha ha ha.

Augh—my mother. She thinks she's *sooo* funny. Sometimes she is. But mostly she isn't. And when I was thirteen, she most definitely was *not* funny. In fact, she was as sour as a pickle. Mostly because she and my dad were always bickering. They fought about everything. About me. About Herr Pomplun's dogs. About my father's mother, my *oma* Anneliese. Oma and my mother don't get along. "Frau Anneliese," my mother says to my father whenever Oma calls, handing him the phone with such distaste you'd think it were injected with the Ebola virus.

And my parents even argued about my bat mitzvah. Traditionally it's a life-affirming, joyous event, right? But not for my mother. She was preparing it with such a vengeance, it looked like World War III might break out any second right in the middle of our kitchen. I mean, you should see how crazy she gets when she organizes a simple ten-guest Passover Seder. Well, she wanted to invite a *hundred and fifty* people to the bat mitzvah.

"A hundred and fifty! You've got to be kidding!" my father said when he heard that.

"I'm not getting married, Mom!" I said.

"Exactly," said my mother. "People can get married a dozen times. But a bat mitzvah is only once. You're telling the world you're grown up and you're part of the Jewish community."

"But I don't believe in God. Why should I be part of the Jewish community?"

That was my mother's cue to roll her eyes and give me one of her withering looks. "Because you're Jewish. That's why."

"Papa's not!"

"You're Jewish. I am, so you are. It's Jewish law."

As if she were an expert in Jewish law! She isn't even religious. Even so, she was always pushing to expose me to as much of Jewish culture as possible. Normally this was no skin off my back because there wasn't much Jewish culture around anyway. I mean, we're talking about *Berlin,* right?

At any rate, if you ask me, my mother was overdoing it when it came to the bat mitzvah. I had to learn Hebrew, memorize a portion of the Torah, write speeches, go to synagogue on the Sabbath, either Friday night or Saturday morning, and on and on.

"It's important for you to stand up and be counted," she said. "You owe it to us. To all the Jews who were murdered."

This, of course, stopped the conversation dead in its tracks. I mean, what was I supposed to reply to that?

"Oh, don't worry," my mother said when she saw me frowning. "The bat mitzvah will be great fun. Just give me two Jews at a table and you've got a barrel of laughs."

"So why aren't we laughing now?" I said.

My mother looked at me as if she wanted to give

me back to the gypsies. But then, after a couple of seconds, she grinned and said, "Hey, that was hysterical, Nelly. Very good. You see, Jews *are* funny!"

Ha ha.

Besides my bat mitzvah, the thing my parents argued about the most was money. Or rather, the lack of it. My mother was always after my dad about not being a famous musician. She was making decent money as a freelancer for a couple of high-paying glossies, but my father's music jobs, except for some steady students he taught, were erratic. Sometimes even nonexistent. Every evening when we sat down to dinner, it was the same old story.

"Anything new?" my mother asked, picking up her steak knife. "Any jobs come in?"

"No," my father said.

"What happened to the job at the Wintergarten?" she asked, aiming her knife and then slitting her meat, drawing blood.

"Nothing. Someone else got it. Someone famous."

"Who?" she asked, raising the meat to her lips.

"What does it matter? You wouldn't know the name anyway."

"If he's so famous why wouldn't I know the name?"

"She," my father said. "It's a she."

My mother almost choked on her meat and some of the blood trickled down her mouth. She loves her meat rare. My father medium. I prefer it well done.

"Someone must need a clarinetist somewhere in Berlin, Benny!" my mother said. "At least you could play at a wedding. Or a bar mitzvah."

My father blanched.

Do you know how people are always using the word *blanched* in novels, but in real life you never really see someone do it? I mean, how often does someone turn white right in front of you? But my father does. Really. Maybe it's a circulation problem. Or something psychological. Or allergic. In any case, you could see his face lose color. And his eyes, which were dark brown, flashed like an exploding supernova.

"Lucy, please!" my father said. "Don't tell me how to do my job."

"He's an artist," I said. "A composer. He belongs on the stage. Or in a recording studio."

My mother slammed her knife down so hard I was afraid for her plate. "I don't care where he is as long as he's earning money being there."

If you ask me, my mother was just too damn tough on my dad. And besides, a good studio job always came along just in the nick of time.

"He doesn't belong in the back room of some synagogue playing klezmer music," I said. "As if it has anything to do with being Jewish anyway. Klezmer has about as much to do with being Jewish as bagpipes have with being Scottish. And he's not even Jewish!"

"Princess," my father said to me softly, "this is

15

between your mother and me."

My mother looked at me and then at my father. "You're not the only artist in this family, Benny," she said. "I'm tired of journalism. I want to write my book."

Her book. Wasn't that just like my mother? For ages she'd been talking about Her Book. A New York Novel, she'd say, whatever that meant. She hadn't even begun it, but she used it as a weapon to shut us up. And it never failed. Whenever she mentioned Her Book, Her New York Novel, we would immediately feel guilty and fall silent and no one would say a word for the rest of dinner. But if Risa, who lived with us, was at the table, she could probably be counted on to break the silence. She would turn to me, pinch my cheek, and say with her Polish accent, "Bubeleh, why don't you put a smile on that beautiful face?"

Beautiful face? I loved Risa but, boy, she needed an appointment with the eye doctor. At any rate, I'd protest and squirm in my seat, but that wouldn't stop her. "Such a *shayne maidele*. Why all this frowning?" Risa would say.

Risa, who was almost seventy, liked to sprinkle her German with Yiddish. *Shayne maidele*, for instance, means beautiful girl, and *bubeleh* is little grandmother, an endearment for young children, especially girls. Risa never lost her Polish accent even though she had come to Berlin over forty years ago. She came with her husband, Leopold, who she had met

16

in Warsaw after the war. Both had survived the Holocaust miraculously. (Well, how else could you have survived the Shoah if not miraculously?) Ever since Leopold died—I was in the first grade when it happened—Risa's been living with us, although we knew her way before that. I've known her all my life. And my mother has known Risa forever, too. That's because Risa and my grandmother, my mother's mother, Hanna Bloom née Hershkowitz, grew up together in Poland, and when my mother came to Berlin, Risa, who was childless, converted her into her ersatz daughter.

My maternal grandmother, Hanna, and her family were lucky to get out of Poland and off to America before it was too late. But Risa and her parents got stuck in Poland. They survived the war hiding out, in basements and barns, in churches, once even in a hidden cellar under a neighbor's turnip patch. Risa doesn't like to talk about it a lot, so I don't have all the exact facts. If you ask her about the war, she goes straight to the part where she met Leopold Ginsberg, which was *after* they were liberated. He was German. Well, actually he was Polish, but he grew up in Germany, so he felt German, but then the Germans sent him back to Poland and—wait a second. Is this getting too confusing to follow? Are you wondering why everyone's moving around from country to country, back and forth between Poland and America and Germany? Our family's history is fairly circuitous— what can I say? My mother says it's the damn fault of

17

the Germans that it's so complicated. "If the Germans hadn't tried to get rid of us," she says, "we probably would have led thoroughly uncomplicated and boring lives. Just like Oma Anneliese and Opa Hans-Otto."

If my mother were reading this now, or editing it, she'd tell me to stop right here, to end the chapter on this controversial note. "Enough is enough," I hear her saying. "Too much exposition is too much exposition. Get down to the story. Cut to the chase."

Maybe this once I'll take her advice. I mean, I *did* want to tell you all about me and Prince William, right?

2
Universe School

It was a rotten September school day. From the very start.

At breakfast I had to listen to my mother yapping away on the phone to some journalist colleague she would be meeting later anyway. In the background we could hear my father practicing his clarinet. His studio is soundproof so no one else in the building is disturbed when he plays, but he had left the studio door open—which happens a lot.

"Jesus, Benny!" my mother screamed.

My father went on playing. He was probably wearing headphones, listening to a playback.

My mother hung up the phone and turned to me. "I have a meeting at the office later. An emergency. But I'll be back for dinner."

My mother was working part-time as contributing editor to *CinemaScoop*. As the name suggests, it was an entertainment magazine that covered film, television, and media industry trends, and printed celebrity interviews, ninety-nine percent fluff. What could the big emergency be? Julia Roberts twisted her ankle? Steven Spielberg announced bankruptcy?

My mother reached into her pocket. "Here. I drew up my guest list last night."

I stared at her.

"Well, how about yours?" she asked.

"*My* guest list?"

"Surely you're inviting some friends to the bat mitzvah. Nelly, it's in eight weeks. How about Anton?"

"Anton? Why should I invite him?" I said.

"Because he's the rabbi's son." She looked at me a moment. "And Yvonne? How about Yvonne?"

I just stared at my mother. Yvonne Priscilla Cohen? Little Miss Popularity? Ha! Popular with everyone except for me.

I looked down at my English muffin and watched the melted butter trickle down the toasted hills and flood the valleys. The truth of the matter was, I had no one to invite. I knew it. And my mother knew it. I used to have a friend, Fiona Lightfoot, but Fiona's father, who was with Microsoft, transferred back to California a couple of months earlier, and we lost contact. *She* lost contact, to be exact. I e-mailed her, but she never answered. So I was a bit of an

20

outsider. Which suited me fine, but it wasn't easy for my mother, the belle of the ball, having a daughter who'd rather look at the stars in the galaxy than the ones at a gala.

"Nelly," my mother said, taking a sip of coffee, "why do you have to be so contrary?"

I hated it when my mother said that. And she was always saying it, always reminding me that I wasn't making an effort to do what she wanted, be like she wanted me to be, as if everything I did that she didn't like was done specifically just to spite her.

"I really wish you'd take an interest in your bat mitzvah preparations," she added. She gave me one of her penetrating looks and went back to her breakfast—until the sound of the clarinet reached us again. "Damn it, Benny!" she yelled. "I can't hear myself think!" She whipped around to me. Uh-oh. Now she was *really* on my case. "And before I forget: when I get back this evening, I want to see your room cleaned up. It's a mess."

"Stop bossing me around!" I shot up from my seat. My room *was* a mess. But so what? "I'll clean up my room when I clean up my room. And besides, I have Hebrew after school. And then I'm meeting Risa."

I stomped out of the kitchen into my father's studio. Yep, he was wearing his headphones, his back to the door. I stood quietly, listening. He was playing something jazzy, but he was also good at playing classical pieces. He must have felt my presence, because he

21

suddenly turned around and raised one end of the headphones.

"She's on the warpath!" I said.

"Have a good one, princess," he said, blowing me a kiss as I shut the door for him.

I grabbed my jacket, searched my room for my backpack, finally found it on the floor next to my broken telescope, swung it over my shoulder, and left the house. Jeez! Whenever my mother was in a bad mood, she always took it out on me. It made me nuts.

I fished a book out of my backpack and made my way to the bus stop. Out of the corner of my eye I caught a glimpse of some neighborhood street kids, not much older than me, hanging out in front of the old gas station around the corner. They couldn't decide if they were skinheads or punks or just a couple of love parade leftovers. At least that's what it looked like to me. One or two of them had their heads shaved like Mohawk Indians. A really skinny guy with shoulder-length peroxided hair wore chains around his neck and a ring through his left eyebrow. He also had serpent tattoos winding down his arms. There was another one who my mother called the Poet because he was always wearing this light blue denim jacket with stuff written all over it in black marker on the back. I tried to read it whenever I went by, but when I was with my mother, she always made me walk fast. And when I was alone,

I felt self-conscious and impolite stopping and reading.

The street kids suddenly appeared one day this past summer. Apparently they slept in the old gas station. My mother called up the Wilmersdorf county hall to find out when they were finally going to tear down the ruins and build something more practical on the lot, but they kept passing her on to someone else and then someone else, until she got so frustrated she just hung up. "I'm going to write a story about it," she threatened, but never did.

It was warm and sunny outside—thank goodness. The weather in Berlin can sometimes be quite fickle, read "rainy." I don't like the rain, and not just because it's sloppy and wet. I mostly don't like it because it makes my hair even frizzier than it already is. And it's pretty frizzy to begin with. That's why I always pulled it back in a braid. When I grow up, I'm going to move somewhere where it's nice and warm and sunny all year round. Like Puerto Rico. The humidity might frizz my hair, but at least I'd have a warm climate *and* access to the giant Arecibo radio telescope. Or maybe Uncle Bruce and Aunt Debbie will die in a tragic car accident and I'll inherit their condo down in the Florida Keys.

"That's a terrible thing to say," my mother said when I joked about it one day. "And anyway, just in case something *did* happen to them, *I'm* inheriting it first. If you clean up your room, though, I'll let you come visit me."

Sometimes, you see, she *can* be funny.

The 110 bus came. It was stuffed to capacity downstairs, so I climbed up the steps to the top level, where most of the kids from my school sat. I was a student at Mark Twain, a public bilingual school, half German, half American. A bunch of the kids came from embassy and celebrity backgrounds, but most of the students were from normal Berlin families and American families that were living abroad.

I reached the top level and almost lost my balance when the bus jerked forward. Some kids laughed at me, and I heard someone call out, "Nerd!" I may, though, have only imagined the "nerd." When you're an outsider like me, your imagination sometimes runs wild. I smiled at Philine Lehnert, who I've known since nursery school days, but she pretended not to notice me. We had once been ice-skating partners in kindergarten. A century ago, it seemed.

I sat down at the first available seat, one seat behind and across from two of the older kids, Bernd Ruppel and Ulla Opitz. And, boy, were they going at it. And in *front* of everybody. Ulla's blazer was open. And when I looked harder, I could tell that her blouse was unbuttoned as well. Bernd's hands were all over her. And then they disappeared behind her. And then they were back up front again. I could see Ulla's hands running up and down Bernd's back, pushing him against her. The two of them were kind of rocking back and forth, too. And kissing. Tongue kissing. I remember sitting there, wondering if it was hard coordinating all that action, and how you learned how to do it. Or did it just come naturally? I supposed it did, but it looked rather complicated all the same. I mean, they were just doing so *much*.

I couldn't help thinking about it.

My eyes darted around the bus and settled on Michael Happe. What would it be like to kiss him passionately? When we'd played spin-the-bottle at Fiona Lightfoot's going-away party last June, we'd kissed. But it was a fleeting event, just a peck on the lips, and salty from the popcorn we'd been eating. In other words: disappointing.

Michael turned to me as if he'd been reading my thoughts. He smiled and his new braces reflected the light. Hmm. Braces seemed like too big of an obstacle for someone like me. An inexperienced kisser might get her tongue caught in the metal clasps or something. Nah. Michael Happe was not the One—at least not yet.

And Uwe Franke, who was sitting in front of Michael? I closed my eyes and tried to visualize our lips touching, but I just couldn't. How could I kiss someone who doodles all day long, filling his note-books with pictures of swords and hatchets, fighter planes and tanks, bombs and exploding human limbs? He'd wrench my neck when he kissed me.

Danny Diller from Los Angeles, whose mother was a singer with the Deutsche Oper, was blowing pink bubbles with his gum a few rows in front of me to the left. Danny was a terrific George in Thornton Wilder's

Our Town, which the theater club put on last year. When he knelt down to say goodbye to his young wife Emily as they lowered her coffin into the earth, I cried. He really made me cry! That's how good he was. My mother, Dr. Lucy, armchair psychiatrist, said that Danny's father died a few years ago of prostate cancer and that he was probably projecting his own feelings of loss onto George's character. Wasn't it just like my mother to spoil it for me? I mean, there I am, thinking Danny is the most brilliant actor I know, and there she is, making him out to be a basket case. But he *was* a good actor. And I bet he was a good kisser, too.

I wondered what it would be like to kiss Danny, to kiss him passionately. Would his lips be soft? Moist? Warm? All of that? None of that? Maybe salty? Or sweet from the bubblegum? And his tongue? What would he do with his tongue? I bet he'd slide it into my mouth and flick it around until it found my tongue. The tongues would play around with each other. Or what if he had bubblegum in his mouth? What if he made a bubble form between our mouths, making it get bigger and bigger? What if I couldn't break away because he was holding me too tight? Maybe I wouldn't be able to breathe. The bubble would get bigger and bigger, as big as a soccer ball and then … *pop!* It would burst all over me, all over my face—pink, slimy, sugary goo sticking to my hair, dripping down along my cheeks, stuffing up my nostrils.

Suddenly, the bus driver put on the brakes. I gasped, emerging from my daydream. I was relieved that all that pink slime was just a figment of my far too vivid imagination. I looked around to see if anyone had heard me gasp. It didn't look like it. My eyes fell on Bernd and Ulla, who were still in a clinch. Bernd saw me staring at him. "Get lost!" he said.

"What are you looking at?" Ulla hissed at me.

As I dropped my eyes to my book, I heard someone say, "Hey, Nelly, taking notes on Ulla for your next science fair project?"

It was Yvonne Priscilla Cohen. She was sitting two rows behind me on the left side of the bus with her two German sidekicks, Nicole Kindler and Caroline Ludwig. My mortal enemies. We were all in the same eighth-grade class, although they were a year older than me.

Yvonne's father was the assistant cultural attaché to the American embassy, but the way she carried on, you'd think he were the president of the whole United States. As far as I could tell, all she had to her name were big breasts, a little brain, and an MCM shoulder bag. Before Fiona went back to America, we swore we would never be caught dead with any of those four items.

"So what are you reading, Nelly?" Yvonne asked. She said it kind of singsongy, so I knew she was teasing me. Nicole and Caroline giggled.

"*A Brief History of Time,* by Stephen Hawking.

Have you read it?" I said.

Of course they hadn't. They just stared at me. Then Yvonne giggled, shaking her head. Her hair swayed from side to side as if a gentle wind were caressing it. She had very straight, glossy, voluminous blond hair that was cut to perfection all the way around in one blunt layer like Prince Valiant. Not one hair was out of place. It was very intimidating.

"Hawking's a brilliant physicist," I said. "He explains the origin and nature of the universe in such a way that it's not hard to understand. Even the most questionably intelligent readers can catch a glimpse of the complexity of our cosmos. I recommend it highly." I smiled and submerged myself in the book.

Although I wasn't looking, I could tell that Yvonne and her friends were unclear as to whether I was making fun of them or not. (Well, what do you think?) I heard Yvonne say, "Nelly is so peculiar. So odd." The words stung, but that was the last I heard, because when I read, I read. I just block everything else out of my brain. Good riddance.

A few minutes later, laughter drilled its way back into my consciousness. It was Yvonne and her friends, and they were pointing out the window at Pia Pankewitz, who was running to catch our bus. Although I wouldn't have laughed, I have to admit it looked funny. That's because Pia's a little overweight, and when she runs, her chubby arms and legs go flailing in all directions.

Pia climbed into the bus, and a few moments later, she appeared up on the top deck. Out of breath, she slowly made her way down the aisle, her eyes searching the rows. When she saw me, her face lit up. Oh, no! Why hadn't I kept my eyes glued to my book? Pia was even more of a loser than I was. When they were passing out brains, they stuffed her head with cotton candy instead of gray matter. At least that's how it seemed to me. And what a schmoozer. The whole day long, yada yada yada.

But just my luck, she sat down right next to me. I decided to read and pretend I hadn't seen her so she wouldn't feel encouraged to start up a conversation. It seemed to work, but then a couple of blocks later, I heard a voice.

"Who do you think is cuter?" Pia said.

I looked up, startled. "Excuse me?"

"Who's cuter. Anton Weissenberger or William?"

"Cuter?"

"Yes," she said. "As in 'more adorable.' Anton or William?"

"William? William who?"

"William *who*?"

I looked at her. And she at me. I could tell she was astonished by my ignorance, but there was nothing I could do about it. I had no idea who she was talking about. After a moment of awkward silence, I returned to my book.

A minute or two later, feeling guilty, I looked up

to see how Pia had taken the rejection. But she had forgotten all about me. Her mouth open in amazement, eyes squinting, she was intent on watching Bernd Ruppel and Ulla Opitz.

The first news of Princess Diana's tragic car accident reached me during lunch in the cafeteria that noon. It's a mystery to me that I hadn't heard about it sooner—Diana had, of course, already been dead thirty-six hours. In any case, even that noon the significance of the news seemed irrelevant. A death in the British royal family? So what? To everyone else, though, it was as if their favorite neighbor had just died. "Oh, she was so beautiful," I heard the girls saying. "A real princess ... and such a dedicated mother... Poor William will be devastated, absolutely heartbroken... Sweet little Harry's still just a boy ... but William, so sensitive. Just like his mother... He looks like her, too... That smile ... those eyes. The way they look up at you."

I couldn't stand listening to all the silly chatter, so instead of hanging out in the cafeteria and subjecting myself to the girls' tears over Little Orphan Harry and bigger orphan William, I decided to take a walk around the campus before my next class.

I was glad to leave the smell of pea soup and cheap perfume behind me. I opened up my book, *Black Holes, White Dwarves, Smart Kids,* but couldn't concentrate. I felt so apart from things. That morning in math class, for instance, I was the only one who'd figured out the bonus algebra question. That's not something that makes you popular, is it? Or take gym. When teams were chosen, they always left me out—and rightly so. Our school was known for its team sports, but *me* play on a team? Sometimes I think I'm a born klutz. My father says that's ridiculous, that physically I'm just a late bloomer. My mother says, "Bloomer schmoomer. She's lazy. *And* she has two left feet." I don't know. Somehow I just don't seem able to muster the right amount of ambition to do anything physical. Like dancing. The girls in school were always swinging their hips to some secret music they had in their heads. But dancing made me feel so self-conscious. Although once, when I was sleeping over at Fiona Lightfoot's house, Fiona and Fiona's sister Phoebe and I danced until something like two in the morning to old Beatles songs we found in their parents' collection. It was very exhilarating. We were already in our nightgowns, and then Fiona and Phoebe put on their Doc Martens and started clunking away. It looked so funny! Long, flowery nightgowns and Doc Martens. I tried them on, too. They were heavy on my bare feet, but then I pretended I was an astronaut in special gravity boots walking on the moon's surface.

Fiona and Phoebe are gone now, clunking their way across Silicon Valley.

"Hey, Nelly!" a voice cried out. I automatically turned to look and *whooosh*—a soccer ball smashed right into the fence in front of me. I jumped.

31

It was Anton Weissenberger, Rabbi Weissenberger's son, exactly two years and four months older than me. My mother is an old friend of his mother's, Bella Metzger-Weissenberger. They met at an anti–cruise missile demonstration, and since my birth a year later, it's been the greatest passion of their lives to get me and Anton together. God knows why. Right from the start it was evident we would never be a unit.

One of my first memories ever is of Anton. I was three, Anton was five, and we were splashing around in a kiddie pool that had been set up in the Weissenbergers' garden. I still see him: a tall, thin, tan boy with curly dark hair and a pair of Batman bathing trunks, whizzing down the slide, trying to knock me over and laughing his head off when he did.

And there was Anton now, laughing his head off in the middle of the Mark Twain soccer field because a soccer ball crashing against a chainlink fence startled me.

This was someone I should invite to my bat mitzvah?

Anton had changed a bit over the years. He was still a tall, tanned boy with curly dark hair, but he was no longer thin. At fifteen he had a chest like a burnished shield and arm muscles popping out like Popeye's foe, Bluto. No wonder everyone called him Arnold, as in Schwarzenegger, instead of Anton, as in Weissenberger. It was rumored, though, that he still had an affinity for Batman—in the form of boxer shorts. You'd think that'd be enough to frighten off the girls. But no. Clearly they found him irresistible. But not me. As far as I was concerned, once a bully, always a bully.

"Hey, four-eyes," Anton said from behind the fence.

"Very original, Anton," I said. "Let's put that in *Bartlett's Familiar Quotations*."

"Nerd."

"Oh, you're killing me with your wit."

He slammed the soccer ball against the fence with a sudden movement. I jumped again. The boys behind him whooped.

"You are such a jerk, Anton," I said. "A major asshole."

"A jerk? An asshole? That's not very original now, Nelly, is it?"

I whisked around and walked away. He was right. It wasn't original.

What a rotten September day.

When I walked back to the main school building, I saw Pia Pankewitz on one of the benches waving me over. I wish I could have ignored her, but that would have been too impolite.

"Don't turn around," she said when I got close to her, "but he's looking at you."

"Who?"

"Arnold Schwarzenegger."

"Anton?" I whipped around and looked back at

33

the soccer field. "Augh. He's anathema to me."

Pia's eyes narrowed. "Anna what?"

Oh, Pia and her cotton-candy brain. "Anathema. Someone I abhor."

She still didn't get it.

"Someone I really detest. Despise. Don't like."

"Oh, really? You don't like him? Too bad. I think he likes you."

"Oh, please!" She *had* to be kidding! I shuddered at the thought. "I could never be happy with someone like that. He's immature. And full of himself."

"But he's awfully cute!"

"Cute … ?" Oh, there was that word again. *Cute.* "Well, I'd never go out with him." I said. "I need someone wiser. More complex. Someone who knows the difference between a white dwarf and a black hole."

"Huh?" she said. "You and your black holes. You have a hole in your head!"

I opened my mouth to answer her, but I realized I had nothing to say.

3

The Telescope

Fritz Friedrichsen was nowhere in sight. He was probably in the back of his shop, in the photo lab. I browsed around a moment, walking past cameras and slide projectors, magnifying glasses and microscopes, binoculars, and stopping, finally, at the telescopes. Astro*Fritz has Berlin's largest selection of new and secondhand astronomy equipment. I bet every amateur stargazer within a hundred-light-year radius has been to this store at least on one occasion.

I walked up the telescope aisle. There they were: the Galaxy Newtons, Pentaxes, Celestrons, and Takahashis. My eyes fell on a huge Meade LXD 50. What a beauty!

"Eighteen hundred," said a voice behind me. "Way out of your ballpark."

35

I turned and stood face-to-face with Fritz, a big, jovial guy in his mid-sixties, the man who taught me how to use a telescope, how to take it apart and put it back together again, and how to take photographs with it. But the last few months I'd been a little negligent about astronomy. Hebrew school took up a lot of my time, and then, on top of that, my telescope broke and it wasn't worth repairing. My German grandparents, Anneliese and Hans-Otto Edelmeister, gave me the telescope two Christmases ago. The second I unpacked it on Christmas Eve, I knew it wouldn't last. It was a scrawny little thing, made of plastic. But my grandparents had come all the way from Hanover to present it to me. When I opened it, their eyes shone brighter than Venus. They were so proud of themselves that they had thought of the perfect gift, and yes, it *was* a good idea, if not the best workmanship. I didn't have the heart to say anything except "Oh, it's exactly what I wanted."

But it was an astronomical waste, no pun intended. I knew it. My father knew it. And my mother wouldn't let us forget it. "Typical," she'd say to me in private. "What do they know about telescopes? They've got no taste, no knowledge, and not even the sense to go and ask someone who does."

I stared at the Meade in Astro*Fritz and promised myself that as soon as my stupid bat mitzvah was over and as soon as I got a new telescope, I'd be back at work stargazing.

"That Meade's way too expensive. And too

heavy," Fritz said. "I have something else in mind for you. You're ready for a sophisticated but light piece of equipment." He walked around to the next aisle and pointed to two aluminum cases. It took about five minutes for him to assemble the telescope, and when he was finished, I was standing in front of a Vixen GR-114 M.

Fritz handed me the instruction manual and a color flyer with a picture of the model. "Take a look at it when you get home. Show it to your parents. I can give you this for about seven hundred. A special price for you."

"Seven hundred marks?" I said. "I might as well open up a Club Med on Mars."

Fritz shrugged. I looked at my watch—and ran off. I was late! Again.

"Edelmeister! I am not standing for tardiness in my class!" said Wladimir Kasarow, my Hebrew teacher, as I slipped into my seat. He muttered something in Russian which I didn't understand, but the two Russian kids in the class, Mikhail Ostrovskij, whose bar mitzvah was one week after mine, and Agness Sigalova, the only other bat mitzvah girl in the class, *did*. Agness was so shocked by the remark, she had a sneezing fit. I avoided Kasarow's eyes and stared ahead at the Playmobil dollhouse across from me on the top shelf of the bookcase. On Fridays and Saturdays during Sabbath services, the classroom was converted into a nursery for the worshipers' children.

"In less than two months you are having your bat mitzvah. How are you to be expecting to read your Torah portion and chant the haftarah when you are not working on your Hebrew?"

Uh-oh. Wladimir Kasarow could go on and on like this for another hour if we were lucky.

"Why are not you looking at me?" he wanted to know.

If he'd glanced into a mirror, he would've known why. Wladimir Kasarow had wads of wild hair growing out of his ears and his nostrils, a wart on his right cheek sprouted more hair, and his eyebrows were one long bushy gray line. I fought the urge to laugh.

"Are you practicing this week at least one mitzvah?" he asked me. Before I could answer, he addressed the whole class. "What is a mitzvah?"

Everyone looked down.

He's got to be kidding. Why does he torture us by repeating these things over and over again? *Everyone* knows what a mitzvah is.

"Rosenstock?" Wladimir Kasarow pointed at David Rosenstock, one of the German bar mitzvah boys.

"A mitzvah is ... well, it's something we do because ... because God ... uh ... God said ... well..." said David, his voice trailing off.

Augh. Everyone except *David* knows what a mitzvah is.

"A mitzvah is a sacred obligation, a commandment," roared Wladimir Kasarow like God on Mount

Sinai. "When we are becoming bar or bat mitzvah, it is meaning we are old enough to do mitzvot."

For the boys, "old enough" was thirteen, but for the girls, it was often twelve. I, though, was celebrating American-style, just a couple months after my thirteenth birthday.

Kasarow looked at all of us, and then he targeted me again. "Edelmeister. You are practicing what mitzvot this week?"

I felt my stomach do a quadruple somersault. I had completely forgotten about my mitzvah. It's a good thing I had a brain the size of the *Encyclopaedia Britannica*. It immediately clicked into its built-in search engine.

"I'm performing the mitzvah of *hidur penei zakein*," I said a few seconds later. "Honoring the elderly."

Wladimir Kasarow just stared at me.

"After Hebrew school, I'm going to visit two very old and very sick women," I said.

Wladimir Kasarow arched his one long bushy eyebrow. "And what are you to be doing?"

"I'm bringing them some good, hot, healthy food. And then we'll talk."

"About?"

I swallowed hard. I didn't relish lying. "God. We talk about God."

I watched Rosi Goldfarb raise her frail but meticulously manicured hand. She wanted to fling the card, but she had no strength, so she just let it drop. An ace of hearts. Trembling uncontrollably with Parkinson's, her hand fluttered back to the table like a butterfly, the rapid movement making the countless liver spots appear as a brownish smear.

Frau Lewi, Frau Goldfarb's best friend, raised her last *doppelkopf* card.

"The queen of diamonds?" I said.

Frau Lewi's eyes narrowed. "How did you know?"

"She's got an IQ of 148, Frau Lewi," Risa said. "It's got to be good for something."

Pouting, Frau Lewi threw her queen of diamonds on the table and then picked up a soggy French fry from a McDonald's box. She popped it into her mouth. "Don't tell me *you* have the queen of clubs, Nelly? Again?"

I did. And I played it.

"Good job, bubeleh," Risa said to me, smiling triumphantly. "We won again!" She threw her ten of spades on the table and gathered up the cards.

"Frau Goldfarb!" said Frau Lewi. "Why'd you save the ace to the end? You had plenty of time to get rid of it before!"

"Ladies, no squabbling," said Risa, hunched over the score pad, calculating her win.

"Frau Ginsberg," said Frau Goldfarb, "how many times do I have to tell you to sit up straight? Your back is going to turn into a question mark."

Sometimes, after Risa and I would visit Rosi

Goldfarb and Helena Lewi, I wondered if maybe I should aim for a career in geriatrics or medical research instead of cosmology. I'd like to discover an elixir of youth. Someone's going to do it someday, so why not me? It drove me crazy the way old people's minds were still charged with energy but their bodies had long since fizzled out.

It took a while for me to get used to it. It's a little scary when people get that old. They have this smell. I used to think it was their medicine, but now I think it's just age. And their skin is so thin, you think every time they move, a bone's going to break through it. The skin on Frau Goldfarb's hand had so many wrinkles, so many bumpy veins, I felt a strong need in her presence to pull it up as I would an ill-fitted sock. Her legs, though, were surprisingly shapely. She owned a dozen pairs of high heels to show them off, even though when she wore them she toddled like a sparrow learning to walk.

Helena Lewi, on the other hand, sat in a wheelchair most of the time. She had serious problems with her hips. She was eighty-two, two years younger than Rosi Goldfarb. And very big. "A whale of a woman," she always said and then laughed until she was gasping for air like one of those stranded giant whales off the coast of Maine I saw one summer. Both she and Rosi had once been Risa's customers when Risa was a dressmaker. But now Risa was their scorekeeper.

Risa's hand moved quickly across the pad. Her

fingers were long and thin and very crooked—the way I imagine the wicked witch's hands in Hansel and Gretel. Or even better: like E.T.'s. Arthritis had bent Risa's fingers terribly out of shape, yes, but it didn't seem to matter. She was a quick scorer. And you should see her chop onions. She was so fast, her eyes didn't even have time to tear up from the onion fumes. And she chopped a lot. In fact, Risa was arguably one of the greatest cooks on the planet. Nonetheless, when she played cards, junk food was de rigueur.

I got up and started throwing the empty junk food wrappers away.

"Why are you always blaming me if we don't win?" Frau Goldfarb said to Frau Lewi.

"Shhh!" said someone behind us. It was Frau Silber. We were not alone in the recreation room. A bunch of residents were down here doing everything from weightlifting and sewing quilts to watching TV. Frau Silber and a bunch of seniors were following the news on the television. A reporter was interviewing Lady Di mourners in front of Kensington Palace.

"Ah, the princess," Rosi Goldfarb said solemnly, standing up and wobbling a bit on her high heels. She leaned over to see if Risa was calculating the card game correctly.

"I always suspected her life would end tragically. She was too thin," said Helena Lewi. With a quick hand movement she rescued the last two remaining

42

French fries from the box I was about to throw away. "Imagine voluntarily starving yourself to death."

"Maybe that's what *you* should do," said Rosi Goldfarb.

"A toothpick, but a beauty nonetheless," said Helena Lewi, referring to Princess Di and ignoring Frau Goldfarb. "Though not as beautiful as our little Nelly." She blew me a kiss.

Ha. Ha.

"Bubeleh, you have such beautiful, thick, dark curls," Risa said, agreeing with Frau Lewi.

"Beautiful curls?" I said. "I want straight hair. Straight, sleek, blond hair. I want hair that sways back and forth like a cornfield when I move my head. Hair that glistens like a mirror. That—"

"We get the picture," said Risa, surprised at my poetic verbosity.

I said it as if it were something I had given much thought to, but frankly, the statement came as a surprise to me, too. I suppose Yvonne Cohen's hair had had a greater effect on me than I was willing to admit. For a moment I wondered if I would soon be going around slinging an MCM handbag over my shoulder.

"Someday you'll be thrilled to have beautiful thick, dark curly brown hair," said Risa. "Don't hide it in a braid."

"Stop it, Risa!" Really. I loved her, but sometimes she was a broken record.

"Augh!" she said with a dismissive hand movement. She looked at Frau Goldfarb and Frau Lewi, holding up the score pad. "Frau Goldfarb, you owe the pot fifteen marks forty. Frau Lewi, nineteen eighty. I owe three marks thirty. Nelly zero. That's thirty-eight marks fifty for next week's food." She handed me the money and then looked up at the ladies. "How about a round of skat?"

They nodded.

"Don't wait up for me," Risa said, giving me a wink.

I kissed the ladies goodbye. Risa gave me an extra-big hug and I smelled her perfume, *Je reviens,* and could feel her glass stone right through my jacket. The stone used to belong to her mother and her mother before her. Risa wears it now on a gold chain around her neck. I felt it jabbing my chest.

"Oh, before I go," I said to Risa, remembering suddenly with a pang of guilt what I had said to Wladimir Kasarow in class, "can we talk about something a second?"

"Yes, dear. About what?"

"About God."

"You want to talk about God? For a *second*? Are you sure you can't stretch that to a minute or two?"

I sat down again. "I told my Hebrew teacher that I was practicing a mitzvah by coming here. I told him that I talked about God with you."

"I see," said Risa. "So talk."

"But what about? I don't believe in any of that."

44

"Not to worry, bubeleh. You won't be the first."
Risa leaned forward. "Just behave *as if* you believed,
as if there were a God. Even if you can't believe in
Him, you should do godly things."

I suppose I looked at her blankly, for she felt compelled to embellish. "And then, maybe, something
might happen," she said.

"Like what?"

"You might believe."

"In what?"

"In Him!"

"Oh," I said, unconvinced. "Interesting."

"Frau Ginsberg!" Frau Lewi cried out. "Call off
the horses! What are you? A missionary?"

"*Schätzchen,*" Frau Goldfarb said to me. "Why
are you always frowning? It's not good for your
complexion."

I instantly faked a smile—not because I was worried about my complexion, but because I was happy
for the change of subject.

"There was a time when I was frowning all the
time, too," said Frau Goldfarb. "But I was allowed
to. I was in Auschwitz."

I was back to a frown. The weight of the past—it
could wipe a smile from your face forever.

"Papa, I found the absolute perfect telescope," I
said after taking a bite of my lamb chop.

I admit that it may not have been the right moment to divulge the news, but how was I to know

45

my parents were at the brink of a major crisis? And besides, I actually thought I was doing something constructive by filling the lull in the conversation. My mother had just mentioned that she had spotted her ex-best friend Beate at the supermarket that evening, near the frozen foods, and that they had both pretended not to see each other. And then there was a lull.

"I know the telescope's not cheap," I went on. "But it comes with a T-2 ring camera adapter."

"Wow!" said my dad.

That was sweet of him, because he really had no idea what I was talking about.

"What does it cost?" said my mother.

And wasn't that just like her? *Wham! Bang!* How much? She always goes straight to the heart of the matter.

"Only seven hundred. A special price. Just for me, Fritz said."

"Seven hundred!" My mother dropped her fork. "Seven hundred? Nelly! You can't be serious. I'm sorry, sweetie, but your hobbies are really getting too expensive."

"But it also comes with a filter for sunspots!"

"Nelly, for God's sake!"

"Okay. Then I'll use my bat mitzvah money."

"We said you were going to *save* that money." She threw my father a look.

What did they know that I didn't?

"I got some bad news today at my meeting.

46

CinemaScoop may be folding," my mother said. "And just when I wanted to write my book."

Uh-oh. There was Her Book again. Her New York Novel.

"Now I can't take time off," she went on. "It was my gravy train. Now I'll have to work my *tochis* off at piecemeal jobs. It'll take me forever to find another cushy job like that." She turned to my father. "I'm worried, Benny."

"You're a worrywart, Lucy. You'll find something. You always do."

"But why is it always *me* who has to find something? I'm sick of being the wage earner in this family."

Oh, no. Not *that* broken record.

"That's not fair!" I said. "Papa works!"

My mother pounced on me—figuratively, of course. "Nelly, do you have nothing better to do than referee our arguments?"

"Well, I think *CinemaScoop* is a stupid magazine anyway," I said.

"Nelly." My father's tone was gently admonishing.

"'Nelly,'" my mother said, imitating him. "Jesus, Benny, can't you for once say more than just 'Nelly'? Can't you say, 'Nelly, that was fresh. Nelly, respect your mother. Nelly, watch that mouth'? You and your German antiauthoritarianism! You're all wimps!"

My father turned to my mother. He kept his voice steady. "So it's the Germans again. I was wondering

47

how long it would take for you to smuggle that into the conversation. I suppose it's the Germans' fault too that the magazine's folding."

"You're damn right it is. The Germans know nothing about movie stars. They don't know how to make them. They don't know how to nurture them. And they don't know how to write about them."

I pushed my plate away and got up. My lamb chop was about to make its way back up my esophagus. "Can I be excused?"

"Sit down, young lady," my mother roared.

I sat down.

I think the sound of her own voice frightened her, because when my mother spoke again, she was a thousand decibels softer. "All I'm saying is that until I find another job, or make some sort of decision, we're going to have to be careful with money. All of us. Even me. Now we can't go to New York." She gave my father a sidelong glance. "Or would you like to find some work and help us out here?"

"Lucy," my father said. "Please."

My mother looked at me for a couple of seconds and then, almost gently, she said, "Look, Nelly, I know you want a good telescope. And I want you to have one. But I think if you want one so much, you should work for it. You're old enough. Why don't you consider baby-sitting? If you start saving your money for a telescope, we'll match your earnings. How's that? Fifty-fifty."

"Baby-sit? You want me to baby-sit?" I said, horrified.

"Why not?"

"Why not?" I shouted.

"Yes, why not? Why do you have to be so contrary?"

"Me contrary? Are you aware of how *long* I'd have to baby-sit in order to save enough for a decent telescope?"

I saw my mother's cheeks turn a bright red. (Remember how my father is always blanching when he gets angry? Well, my mother's always flushing.) "What am I?" she screamed. "A bank? The mint? Some jerk who dishes out money at the drop of a hat?"

"It would take me *forever* to get a telescope baby-sitting!"

"You've got all the time in the world. The stars aren't going anywhere."

That was the last straw. I jumped up from my seat and made a beeline for the door.

"I hate her! I hate her! I hate her!" I yelled at the walls as I stomped through the living room to my room. I slammed my door and fell on my bed in tears.

Really, it was absolutely the most rotten day of my life.

wonder

My window was a monster. It climbed three meters high from the floor to the ceiling and stretched five meters across. It was partitioned off into a grid of forty-eight window panes like a checkerboard. It faced north, as most artist's studios do. But now it was my personal observatory window.

My head was all scrunched up and achy, my cheeks hot and taut from my tears. It had been two hours since the fight with my mother. The whole time I just sat gazing out at the giant sky before me, my room shrouded in darkness. The only light came from my computer, from my screen saver with the nine planets of our solar system revolving around the sun. And some light came in from outside, of course, yellow rectangles of light from distant apartments, light from nighttime Berlin, from the sky over Europe, from the moon, the stars, the universe.

I watched some clouds move across the window from right to left like a curtain being pulled across a stage, hiding the moon behind its puffy cloth. And then—*shwhooo!*—the clouds moved off again, disappearing stage right, revealing the moon once more. It must've been pretty windy up there.

The heavens were clear now, but below me, all I could make out was a diffuse, deep blackness. The whole block behind our house, under my window, was divided into garden plots set in neat rows of tidy cottages and trimmed lawns guarded by an army of red-capped, green-suited terracotta gnomes. But after nightfall, it was deserted down there—especially in the fall and winter months. From my window the earth below was little more than a silent, dark, meaningless blob of Nothingness. But above me, high above me, beyond the moon, the clouds, and the wind, behind Venus's brightness, far, far away in the endlessness of the skies, was, I was absolutely sure of it, Everything. Everything that was important, and just waiting, waiting desperately to be discovered.

So I sat there, in my armchair, looking out at the sky. I was trying to remember a dream I had had the night before. Parts of it had suddenly come back to me, but I still couldn't remember what it *felt* like. I hadn't done much in the dream except float, just float peacefully among the stars, drifting past diamonds of light and then more diamonds of light, only to discover more and more of it, room after room, kingdom after kingdom, heaven after heaven of black sky and stars and diamonds and beauty. But it was more than just beautiful. More than just peaceful. What exactly was it? What kept me poised above? What had made me so excruciatingly light? What feeling?

I stared and stared at the stars.

And then, I knew. I remembered.

Wonder. It was wonder. It was the sheer wonder of the universe that had lifted me up, filling me with such weightlessness, such transparent joy I could have drifted on forever.

Oh, to have that dream again. And again.

Knock. Knock.

I turned my head toward the door.

"It's me, princess," I heard my father say.

My father looked around my room for somewhere to sit, but the chairs were piled high with dirty laundry, notebooks, textbooks, papers, cassettes, CDs, you name it. The floor didn't look very inviting, either. The wooden planks were coated with dust, the rug infested with lint and dotted with dirty socks, dog-eared books, and assorted clutter. My mother was right, of course. I really *had* to clean up my room.

My father snapped on my night-table lamp and I saw his movements reflected in the glass of the window. He took a pile of dirty laundry from my swivel chair, dropped it on the bed, and sat down. His eyes were on me. I turned to him.

My dad is handsome. My mother's ex-best friend, Beate, uses the word *attractive* to describe him, but that always makes me laugh because the word reminds me of magnets. "Very attractive," I remember Beate saying. "He's better-looking than Richard Gere, and even Harrison Ford."

My father has dark brown eyes and wavy dark brown hair that's graying at the temples. He's tall and thin, and his shirttails have a way of always slipping out of his pants. Whenever we walk down the street together, women smile at him. And he always smiles back—that is, when my mother's not with us. These days, my father and I still walk around together, but when I was growing up, we used to do it more because my mother worked full-time and it was my father who stayed home and took care of me.

"What do you see out there?" my father asked, gesturing toward the window.

"I don't know."

He didn't look satisfied with my answer.

"Questions maybe," I said. "Lots and lots of questions."

"Like?"

I shrugged. "Like where did it all come from? What was here before? When did it begin? How did it happen? Where's it going? Stuff like that."

My father smiled.

I adored my father's smile. He has very good teeth. They're straight and sparkly, like in a mouthwash commercial. I always thought it was too bad he played the clarinet. His audience never gets to see his teeth.

"I bet someday you'll answer all those questions," my father said, looking at the window. "But maybe you should come back down to Earth first?"

I rolled my eyes. I knew what was coming.

"You hurt her feelings," he said.

"*Her* feelings?"

"All she did was ask you to consider baby-sitting. *Hate* is a pretty strong word."

"She deserved it. She's always nagging. And she's always picking on you. And harping about work."

"You don't have to worry about me, princess. I know how to take care of myself."

Our eyes locked.

"What's the matter?" my father said.

"The telescope."

He shook his head. "There's something else eating you."

The second he said it, I knew he was right. I didn't want them to, but suddenly my eyes swelled with tears.

"What is it, honey?"

"Papa, am I … odd?"

"Odd?"

"The kids in school … they look at me sometimes as if … as if I were from another planet or something."

"Did they say which one?"

"Papa!" I said, swatting at him. "At least *you*

should take me seriously."

"Oh, princess, I do. I do," he said. "Look, there's nothing wrong with being different or unconventional. I'm a musician. I thrive on it. But if you're uncomfortable standing out from the crowd, maybe that means you should try to focus on how you're similar to the other kids."

"I do. I really do. But then, I don't know, somehow our heads don't click."

"Then don't use your head. Just listen to them. Try to understand where they're coming from. Feel it. You're probably not that different."

I got out of my armchair and hugged my father. "I'll try," I said.

"I know you will." He kissed my forehead lightly.

"I love you, Papa."

"Ditto, princess."

And then, after a moment or two, he said softly, very very softly, "Come—come say good night to your mother."

"Dodi. What kind of name is that for a princess's millionaire lover?" my mother said. She shook her head. "It's all Charles's fault, you know. He made her crazy. He drove her mad."

"Don't be silly, Lucy," Risa said, lifting her peppermint tea to her lips without taking her eyes from the television screen. "She died in a car accident, not in an insane asylum."

The living room was charged with flashing blue light from the television. I sat down between Risa and my mother on the green suede sofa. My father lurked in the shadows. He couldn't decide if he wanted to sit down or not.

"I'm sorry," I said to my mother.

"That's nice," she said, barely taking her eyes from the screen. "What for?"

"What *for*?" I couldn't believe it. Was I *that* unimportant?

My mother laughed, put her arm around me, and squeezed me. "You are such a silly goose. I'm only joking." She kissed the top of my head. "I'm sorry, too, sweetie." She took my hand and turned back to the television. "The poor girl never had a life of her own. Especially not with that witch of a mother-in-law."

"I'm going to my studio to practice," my father said. "Tell me when some real news comes on."

The television was full of Princess Di: Diana, a timid kindergarten teacher in cashmere surrounded by dribbling toddlers; Diana, a blushing bride in white lace being given in marriage to Charles; Diana in jungle fatigues embracing children lamed by mine bombs; athletic Diana skiing; partygoing Diana at a state function; anorexic Diana jogging; shy Diana; angry-at-the-paparazzi Diana; smiling-at-the-people Diana; Diana the princess; Diana the wife; Diana the goodwill ambassador; Diana the dutiful daughter-in-law. Suddenly, the presenter's voice-over died out and sob story music came up. And there she was: Diana the mother, heavily pregnant. And then: Diana the mother with infant William, with infant Harry and toddler William, with schoolboy William, with William and Harry at the races. At a picnic. The music increased in intensity. And there are the boys without Di. At five and three. At ten and eight. At thirteen and eleven. And there's William at thirteen. At fourteen. At fifteen. At … oh … William. *William?* Is *that* William Windsor? Is *that* the future king of Great Britain? My God, Hans Christian Andersen himself could not have created a more perfect prince. Why, he's so … so … what was the word I was looking for? … so … cute. That's it. Yes, cute. As in adorable.

And that smile. Just like his mother's.

But how heart-wrenching. The poor boy. The poor, poor sweet orphan. He has no one to care for him now. No one to kiss him good night. No one to mend his socks.

"Nelly?" I heard my mother say.

I couldn't answer. A comet had fallen on my head, cracked open my heart, sucked the breath out of me. I felt faint.

"Nelly?" my mother said. "Are you okay?"

I was fine.

I was sick.

I was … in love.

In love. Finally. After all these years.

What a wonderful September day.

5
Smitten

It was the grandest likeness of the prince I had yet to come upon. It was life-size. Hug-size. Kissable. You can't imagine the excitement I felt every time I flipped through *Girl Zone* magazine and the pinup unfolded before my eyes. Wills somersaulted to the floor, landing softly, miraculously, on his perfectly polished oxblood wingtips. There he was: the Future King. His hair slightly mussed. His eyes as blue as an azure sky. His smile a soft whisper. He stood there, looking back at me in a three-piece, dark blue, pinstriped suit, its fabric so lush I knew it must be part cashmere. His jacket was unbuttoned, revealing its matching vest, a lighter-hued blue shirt the color of his eyes, double-stitching at the collar, a ruby red silk tie. A ruby red kerchief garnished his breast pocket. His left arm hung relaxed at his side; his right hand was hidden in the right pocket of his trousers.

I don't know how long we stared at each other.

I was smitten.

"Nelly!" my mother called.

I could hear my mother's leather pumps coming toward me fast. I didn't have time to turn off my computer, but before she knocked, I managed to fold up the poster and slip it back between the pages of *Girl Zone*.

"Nelly?" my mother said, swinging the door open. Her head popped in. "We're going in ten minutes. Are you ready?"

Of course I was ready. I was always ready to spend two gruesome hours boring myself to death in synagogue. The bar and bat mitzvah kids *had* to go to Sabbath service—it was mandatory.

"I'm coming," I said sullenly, slipping a belt into the loops of my jeans.

My mother's eyes narrowed. "What? You don't own a skirt? And what's with the sneakers?"

Oh, no. Now she was off on one of her tangents.

"At least you could have gotten dressed up for Risa. How do you think she feels going to shul with you looking like a bum? Don't you—" My mother stopped midsentence when she saw *Girl Zone* lying on the floor. "Since when do you read teen magazines?"

"I don't," I said, which was the truth. Who could read all that garbage with a straight face, all that

"Help! How do I get rid of the pimples on my back?" and "Dear Jana, Is it true that boys only like big breasts?" Or my very favorite: "My boyfriend never calls me. We never go out together. He's not interested in my hobbies. Should I break up with him? Sincerely, Coco."

"Someone gave it to me," I answered as nonchalantly as I could.

"I suppose there's a royal pinup in it?" my mother said, amused.

My cheeks got all tingly, as if they were going to break out in a rash. I whipped around and went to my closet, pretending to look for a change of clothes. No way was I going to let her see me blush.

My mother picked up the magazine. "What's it doing on the floor? That's where it belongs," she said, chucking it on my desk, where *Batty Patty's Prince William Page* was displayed on my computer. A photo of the prince, blinking on and off, attracted her attention. And that's when she cracked her now famous joke, "love at first site."

Ha ha.

My mother walked over to the computer and squinted into it. I was sure she was going to mock William's blinking picture, but then she said, "Are you still online? Oh, Nelly. You've been blocking the phone for over an hour. It's a waste of money. And besides, I have to make a call."

I didn't answer her. I just stared ahead. She really hates that.

She waited for me to respond, but when I didn't, she said, "Well, hurry up. We're going to be late."

"Late?"

She gave me one of her withering looks. "Yes. Late." And off she went.

To Lucy Bloom-Edelmeister, being late meant you didn't get to synagogue early enough to be seen by everyone and their grandmother before fading into the anonymity of the congregation. Clearly, being seen was the single most important reason for going to synagogue.

I listened to my mother's pumps *click-clack* their way back down the hall and across the living-room parquet to the front hall. Then I turned to the mirror above my dresser. I did Risa a favor and tried to flatten out my bangs. Then I kicked off my sneakers and put on a pair of loafers for her, too. Mission accomplished, I opened *Girl Zone* and beheld the prince.

The best part of the picture was the tiny little blond hairs running down the nape of William's neck. I chanced upon them one day while doing a homework assignment for art class. I was scanning the poster with a magnifying glass, examining its multicolor dot matrix, when I discovered wisps of soft fuzz ablaze with backlight along William's neck. To me, those tiny little hairs made William seem so vulnerable, so needy. I wanted to reach out and stroke his cheek, cradle him, tell him that everything was going to be okay. "I know you miss your mother. But the hurt will go away. And maybe, one fine day, you'll be able to open

61

yourself up to someone else. Let me hold you and make you feel better," I'd say to him.

I went to the mirror and practiced the sentence with a British accent. A friend of my father's, Grant Neville, a bass player, is Australian. He told me if I want to sound British, I should talk as if I have popcorn in my mouth.

I watched my cheeks fill out with imaginary popcorn. "I know you miss your mother," I said to the mirror. "Let me make you feel better."

I looked at my poster. Everyone in the house already knew about Prince William, so I might as well hang it up. I took down the flyer with the Vixen telescope that was hanging on the inside of my closet door, pinned it on the wall next to my mirror, and hung Prince William up on the door instead. Now when I opened the door, I was standing right in front of him. He'd have to bend down just a little to kiss me, but well, so? That's how it was in real life, wasn't it?

I went to my computer. It used to belong to my mother. She had named it Bubbe, which means grandmother in Yiddish. When my mother was a little girl, her *bubbe* used to tell her wonderful turn-of-the-century tales about Russia and New York.

"Your great-grandmother Naomi was a great storyteller and a grand lady," my mother was always saying. "She was extremely poor and had to work her fingers to the bone her whole life, but she was a strong woman and brought up four healthy, happy children. She was lucky to get out of Europe before it was too late."

Some of Bubbe's family, like Risa's, were not so lucky, because when they wanted to get out of Europe, either they didn't have the money for the passage, or it really *was* too late. Bubbe's uncle Mosche, her aunt Mimi, and three cousins and their families were all murdered in concentration camps. But Bubbe herself lived a long life. She died in Flatbush, Brooklyn, of old age just a year before I was born. They named me after her. They took the *n* from Naomi and made me a Nelly.

I stared at Bubbe, the computer. If it weren't for her and the Internet, I wouldn't know as much about William as I did. The school library had been a substantial source of data on British history, and the girls' magazines, on the royals, but the Internet was by far the most convenient and original place to find information. And sitting at home with Bubbe in front of me, I could write William e-mails, too. I actually wrote a few and even put them through my computer's spell checker, but I didn't send them. The temptation was great, but in the end the thought horrified me. In fact, I removed them from the out basket because I was afraid I might forget and accidentally mail them. And then what! Besides, I wasn't even sure that e-mails were the best contact method. The only way for a nonroyal like myself to gain Wills's attention was to stand out from the crowd, I felt. I'd have to do something so astounding that he'd want to seek me out. What if, for instance, I made an awesome discovery?

I'd already been to Potsdamer Platz, to the State Library, looking for university catalogs from England, Wales, and Scotland to see if I could study astrophysics there. Apparently I could, so I figured that might be the answer. At the very latest I'd meet Prince William when I became valedictorian of my graduating class at Oxford. I could see myself years hence calling up William at Buckingham Palace and personally inviting him to the commencement exercises at my school. "Nelly Sue Edelmeister?" he'd say. "Why, of course! I read about you in the *Times* the other day. You researched black matter in globular clusters by using gravitation lenses. Yes, I'd love to come by and be a part of your graduation celebration. Globular clusters have always been my secret passion."

But it would take a while before I could study at Oxford. Maybe I should try to figure out another way of getting William's attention, something that could possibly happen within the next few weeks, or at the latest by the following spring, let's say...

"Nelly!" my mother called. "Are you coming or what? We're waiting."

I turned off Bubbe and readied myself for the morgue—I mean synagogue.

I leaned back in my seat. The synagogue's wooden pew was not the most comfortable, but the cantor's song and the congregation's chanting were lulling me to sleep. I closed my eyes and imagined myself floating, exhilarated, while in the distance a figure glided toward me. It was Prince William wearing his three-piece, dark blue, pinstriped, cashmere-blend suit. Poised before me, he smiled and then took me in his arms. Our hearts soaring, we drifted from star to star...

"Nelly!" my mother said, poking me softly with her elbow. "Listen."

I jerked up to the sound of the cantor singing.

My mother's face was aglow. She adored the chanting in the synagogue, the blowing of the shofar, Hanukkah songs, *Fiddler on the Roof*, Barbra Streisand, anything vaguely Jewish-sounding. "The chanting reminds me of home. Of Brooklyn," she always says. "It reminds me of all the times Bubbe used to drag me to shul when I was a kid. The cantor was like a superstar to those immigrants. The rabbi was the leader, yes, he was the moral authority, but the cantor—oh, he was something else. He captured the hearts of the ladies. They loved him. Like Frank Sinatra. Or John Lennon. Like Robbie Williams. You should have seen the ladies in their shawls and babushkas, the way they swarmed around the cantor after the service. Like bees buzzing around a glass of warm Coca-Cola. You should have seen them swoon when he sang."

I turned to Risa. She didn't appear to be swooning over Cantor Morgenstern. And neither were Frau Goldfarb or Frau Lewi. Cantor Morgenstern was short and stocky and almost as old as Frau Lewi and Frau Goldfarb. But his voice was still strong. Sometimes, when I went downstairs to the ladies' room in the basement, I could still hear his voice. And he had a headful of thick hair. It was all white and wild. Like Einstein's. I stole another glance at Risa. Even if she wasn't swooning over him, maybe she was still Cantor Morgenstern's type.

Risa felt my eyes on her. She looked up. "They never stop talking," she said, gesturing to the congregation. "They don't even shut up for the Kaddish!"

The service was reaching its finale. The Kaddish, a prayer in memory of the dead, is always recited toward the end of the service. It's a pretty solemn affair, but you couldn't tell from this synagogue. In fact, my father always gets a kick out of coming to synagogue because it's so noisy. Babies cry, kids run around screaming, and everyone's laughing and schmoozing with their neighbor. It's a social event, a party, a fashion show, not a time for a quiet conversation with God. "In church you can hear a needle drop," my father always says, "but here you wouldn't even hear a bomb."

"God forbid!" Risa says, lifting her eyes heavenward.

But who has to worry about a bomb? To get in here, you have to walk through one of those metal detectors like they have in the airport. "That's so sick," my mother always says, "but what are you going to do? Convert to Catholicism?"

where all the different train lines converge at Grand Central Station. Anyway, when she saw me looking at her legs, she was embarrassed, I think, and said in that self-mocking tone of hers, "Don't worry. In *that* department, you take after your father's family."

At any rate, after that incident in the locker room, my mother always wore one of those Hawaiian-print wraparound skirts to the beach, and she only took it off to take a quick dip—which kind of made me feel bad, if you know what I mean.

The crowd was thinning out in the synagogue courtyard, but my mother was still working on Herr Lerner. The way he looked at her, you could tell he had no idea she had flab under her clothes. She rarely wears tight-fitting clothes anymore, but she had on a black wool suit that accentuated her smallish waist. A white blouse with black-and-white trimming peeked out at the collar and the sleeves. It was very simple, but stylish. Even elegant. I guess some people would call my mother attractive. Some might even go as far as to say she's beautiful even though she has dark, frizzy hair like me and she always wears black. Usually, though, she walks around like a schlepper. Her favorite outfit is baggy black pants; a long, wide, black top with a deep V-neck; and black boots that are too expensive to be called combat boots but look like something straight out of *Saving Private Ryan*. Risa doesn't like my mother leaving the house like that. "You're going to the supermarket, Lucy, not to war. And what's with all the black? Who died?" My mother just laughs and says, "It's the fashion, Risa. And besides, black hides my hips." My mother's ex-best friend, Beate, says my mother's a snazzy dresser. "She looks like a teenager, not like the mother of one," she says. But if you ask me, I'd rather have a mother that looks like a mother than a mother who looks like a tenth grader marching off to war.

"Oh, that sounds interesting!" I heard my mother say to Herr Lerner. A few heads turned toward her voice. Why did she have to be so loud? Why does every sentence out of her mouth puncture the air like a string of caps going off?

"An onscreen reporter?" I heard her say. "Sure I can do that! Do you have the fellow's name and number?"

Augh! My mother was always on. She never gave up. Disgusted, I turned to leave. And who do I bump into?

"My mother said I should say hello to you," said Anton Weissenberger.

I followed his eyes and saw Bella Metzger-Weissenberger, the rabbi's wife, who had now joined my mother and Herr Lerner. She waved at me. And then my mother smiled encouragingly. Ha! Those two should open up a dating service.

"And what else?" I asked.

"And what else what?" said Anton.

"And what else did your mother tell you to tell me?"

"Nothing."

"Good. So now you can go," I said, looking the other way.

Anton, indignant, was only too happy to comply.

On the way out, I saw Yvonne Cohen at the other end of the courtyard. She was with her younger sister, Alison. Yvonne leaned over Alison and whispered something in her ear. It was a very intimate gesture. Very girlish. Then Alison turned to her and took her hands, and they danced together. Yvonne spread her legs and scooped Alison under them and then back up—the way my mother and father sometimes danced when they pretended they were rock-'n'-rolling. The girls' cheeks got all flushed and a few moments later, out of breath, they plopped down on a bench, arm in arm, talking animatedly. For a moment I was actually envious of Yvonne.

The following Monday was the beginning of the end of my Hebrew school career. Wladimir Kasarow caught me red-handed with my *Teen Scene* magazine. He must have been on my case, because normally he's not that attentive. But there was the class reciting from the Tillim, repeating word for word after our teacher, and there I was, reading a story about William and his favorite recipes for his father's home-grown veggies. Suddenly, Wladimir Kasarow's bushy knuckles plunged into my peripheral vision. With one swoop he scooped up my magazine, then held it up in front of the class with his thumb and forefinger, letting it dangle like a dead mouse by its tail. To my mortal embarrassment, the pages fanned open and a pullout pinup of William unfolded, one panel, then another, and another, revealing sneakers, then jeans, then a flannel plaid shirt, then the princely head. Finally we saw William standing there, James Dean–like, leaning against a wall, thumbs in the pockets of his jeans.

Wladimir Kasarow's eyes were surely going to pop out of their sockets and tumble over his glasses. My teacher looked at me with such utter disgust, you would have thought he had caught me drooling over a porno magazine or running around in the nude. And actually, that's how I *felt*, as if I had been stripped, my soul laid bare, my secret discovered, my shame.

"Nelly Sue Edelmeister," he boomed. "I am speaking to your mother. If something like this is happening one more time, you will be leaving my class. Do you understand? You will be out of here!"

I understood.

Kasarow ruined my entire evening. I couldn't stop worrying: had he called my mother or not?

Once in the apartment, I was happy to find myself alone. Risa was visiting Frau Goldfarb and Frau Lewi, and my parents were having dinner at Marianne Wohlers's, a journalist colleague of my mother's. I did my homework, chatted a bit about globular clusters with some astronomy-oriented high school kids in

Nebraska during their lunch break, e-mailed Batty Patty's Prince William site, and then worked on my scrapbook. I cut out the article about William's favorite veggie recipes and pasted it to page forty-three. The book was filling up quickly with photographs and articles from magazines, hard copies of possible e-mails to William, printouts of some websites. I had also become quite an Anglophile, collecting things like the wrapper from Walkers shortbread biscuits and a stamp with a picture of Queen Elizabeth that was on a rejection letter to my father from a London recording studio. I sprayed the pages with some men's cologne I found at the very back of the cabinet in my parents' bathroom. On the faded label, I read ENGLISH LEATHER. And then, before going to bed, I decided to treat myself to a video of a television documentary about Princess Di I had taped. I fast-forwarded it to my favorite part.

And there he was: the prince I had come to cherish like the air I breathe. He was playing soccer. His shirt had *Eton* printed across it. I switched the speed to slow motion and watched the movement of William's body, frame by frame, fascinated by the rippling of his leg muscles...

The room was suddenly flooded with light. Blitz! The living-room door was swung open.

"Oh, I'm sorry," my mother said. "I didn't know you were still awake."

I gulped. Did she, or did she not know about Hebrew school? "You're early," I said.

I watched my mother pull off her earrings and slip out of her shoes. I saw her glance furtively at the television screen and smile to herself when she saw William.

"Boring party," she said. "But I landed your father a gig."

"Thanks, manager," my father said to my mother. "What's your cut?" He turned to me and gave me a kiss. I noticed that he smelled of alcohol. He made a face at me. "They want me to play klezmer. At Ari Landau's daughter's wedding on Saturday." He bowed ceremoniously. "Ladies and gentlemen, introducing the King of Klezmer, Bazooka Benny."

I laughed.

"That's nothing to sneeze at," my mother said. "The Landaus have influential friends and relatives." She plopped down on the couch next to me. "I'm pooped." She opened up her mouth and flashed me a smile. "Do I still have broccoli between my teeth?"

It was too dark in the room for me to see.

My mother called out to my father, "What is it that you Germans love about broccoli? It's as if it were engraved in your collective consciousness. Serve-broccoli-at-dinner-parties-or-die." She turned back to me. "It was even in the dessert. In the ice cream."

"Broccoli?" I asked, shocked.

My father laughed. "That was *mint*, Lucy!"

"Really?" my mother said with feigned astonishment, her eyes twinkling with mischief. "Well, by the way Marianne cooks, who can tell?" She turned to me. "So how was your day?"

I put up my guard. "Fine. My day was fine."

"And Hebrew?"

"The usual." I turned back to the television, holding my breath, waiting for the ax to fall.

"What did you have for dinner?" she asked.

Aha. So Kasarow *hadn't* spoken to her.

I reached for the remote. "Look, Mom, chuck the Q and A. Can't you see I'm working on something?"

I pressed the play button. William's soccer game jolted back to life. Diana was rooting for William.

My mother stared at me a moment, then got up and walked to her bedroom. "I have to brush my teeth," she said.

The walls in Berlin apartments are thick. But if the doors are open, you can hear most everything—if you want to. The door to my parents' bedroom was open a crack. My door, too.

"We have to talk to her," I heard my mother say to my father. "A crush is sweet, but, my God, she's obsessed with that boy."

"And I'm obsessed with you," my father said, or rather *sang*, improvising a tune. "Shu-bi-du-bi-du. Lucy, Lucy Broccoli, love me, love me, love me do."

My mother laughed—unexpectedly loud and happily. I wondered if maybe she had had a little too much to drink, too.

And then I heard nothing.

74

I got up and undressed. And then, suddenly, I heard my father singing again. He has this deep, guttural voice that's a little scratchy at the end of a phrase.

"Oh, Benny, Benny, Benny," I heard my mother say.

I went to my door and closed it. I didn't want to have to hear all *that*.

Maybe I closed the door a little too loudly, because then I heard my mother call out, "Nelly? Nelly? Was that you?"

I didn't answer. Instead, I tiptoed to my door, and when I heard my mother go back in the bedroom and close the door, I opened up my door again a crack.

"This Prince William thing is getting a little out of hand," I heard my mother say.

"It's just a phase, Lucy. Girls go through it."

"But it's getting silly." My mother's voice was loud. Even though their door was closed, I could hear it.

"Maybe that's what she needs. To be silly." My father was getting louder, too.

"Since when are you such an expert on *that* age group?"

I was about to ponder that last statement when I heard my father say, "I'm entitled to know something about my daughter. Who took care of her every day for three years until she went to kindergarten? Who changed her diapers six times a day?

75

And rocked her to sleep? Who picked her up from school every day?"

"Who had *time* to pick her up from school every day because he didn't have a job?"

If my father answered, I don't know. The next thing I heard was the *Harald Schmidt Late Night Show*. That was my father's favorite program.

"All right!" I heard my mother say. "Then *I'll* talk some sense into her!"

Then the sound on the television was gone. My father had probably plugged in the earphones, put them on his head, and blocked out my mother.

I heard the door to their bathroom slam.

A day or two later, I was sitting at my desk with my computer, aka Bubbe, conducting a people search online, trying to find my old girlfriend Fiona Lightfoot, when my mother paid me a visit. She just barged in, bowled me over with a kiss on my cheek, and threw herself down on my bed. I suppose this was the moment she had chosen to "talk some sense into me." In the mirror I could see that her kiss had left a bright red lipstick mark on my cheek. I wiped it off demonstratively.

"Augh. Here's a tissue," she said, pulling a Kleenex out of her pocket. "You don't want to get your lipstick fingers on everything now, do you?"

"Right! You can smudge my cheek whenever you want to, but I have to be pristine clean."

My mother rolled her eyes. "Honey, I'm sorry. I'm

sorry I kissed you." She paused, searching for words. "Do we have to fight about everything?"

I didn't answer her. Her question seemed rhetorical. Instead, I wiped the lipstick off with the tissue, rolled it up, aimed it at my basket, and threw. It missed and landed under the bed.

"This room!" my mother said, taking in the mess.

"Is that what you came in here to talk to me about?"

"I didn't come in here to fight with you." She made herself comfortable on the bed and changed her tactics. "Did I ever tell you that when I was your age I wanted to marry a prince?" She was suddenly all chummy, as if we were best friends exchanging secrets at a pajama party. "Did I ever tell you that I wanted to marry William's father?"

"Prince Charles? How could you have wanted to marry Prince Charles. His nose!"

"All the boys I knew in Brooklyn had noses like that."

"But his ears!"

She laughed. "Yes, his ears are exceptionally large, aren't they? But he was a young man with a big future. What could be wrong with big ears? I wanted to marry him."

"Marry him? Thank God you didn't."

"But let me tell you, young lady, if he'd married *me*, he'd never have gotten into the mess that he's in today."

I laughed. Naturally I'd picked up a load of information about the marital problems between Prince Charles and Wills's dead mom, so I thought my mother's comment was pretty funny. But when I think about it, I wonder why I laughed. My parents had their marital problems, too, and, believe me, it's no laughing matter. And anyway: if my mother *had* married Charles, who's to say she wouldn't have driven him crazy, too?

My mother's face turned earnest. "And you, sweetie? What do you find so appealing about Prince William?"

Questions like that are pretty tricky. I mean, what are you going to say? "He's cute," I said.

"Cute?"

"Yes. As in adorable. Never heard the word?"

"Not out of your mouth. No."

"And like his father before him, he has a big future."

"Really? You call hunting foxes and playing polo a big future? And anyway, you're a young woman with a big future. You don't need him for that."

"Thank you, Ms. Women's Lib."

My mother rolled her eyes.

"And what about you and Prince Charles?" I went on. "I bet *you* really needed him, huh?"

"Nelly, I was infatuated with the guy for a minute and a half. And anyway, you should be spending your time preparing for your bat mitzvah instead of stuffing your head with this nonsense the whole day.

It seems a little silly. Coming from you."

I just stared at her—willing her out of my room.

And it worked.

My mother rose. I heard her luxury combat boots creak. "I've got some work to do," she said. She turned to go, but stopped at the door. I have to say this much for her: she never gives up. "You don't have to be a princess, sweetie," she said, her voice cracking with emotion. "You're going to be a great astronomer."

"Maybe," I said. And I left it at that. I couldn't say any more anyway. If I had, my voice would have cracked, too. She really believed in me, and that made me feel even more terrible—but only for a second, because then she started talking nonsense again.

"It just doesn't make sense," she said, taking a step back into the room. She was standing near my mirror, looking at the flyer of the Vixen telescope I had hung up on the wall. "How can a girl like you, a girl with your brains, waste your time on an illusion?"

I hit the ceiling. "What do brains have to do with this? Do you think Albert Einstein didn't want to go to bed with Marilyn Monroe?"

My mother's mouth literally dropped open.

"It's an infatuation," she finally said.

"No it's not!"

"You'll get over it."

"It's *not* an infatuation!" I screamed.

"Why do you have to be so contrary?"

"I'm *not* contrary."

"William's not going to invite you up for tea and crumpets!"

"That's how much *you* know. Just you wait and see. He'll invite me up. And for *more* than just tea and crumpets!"

"Fine," she said, turning to go. "Fine. But just make sure you clean up your room first, you hear me?"

6

The Goal

"Excellent, Tillie!" Frau Sander, our gym teacher, said, blowing her whistle. "Excellent form. Show us that again."

I looked up to see the tallest girl in the class, Mathilda Lichtenberg, aka Tall Tillie, new at school that year, shoot a free throw. She made it look easy. I knew better.

Basketball was a mystery to me. It was fast. And aggressive. You had the ball, you threw the ball, you lost the ball. There were so many things to think about, ergo to worry about: dribbling, running, throwing, catching, blocking, defending. Believe me, logarithms are easier—even without the chart.

I looked down the line. There were three girls before me and then it would be my turn. Bianca

Neumann managed to get the ball into the basket. Caroline Ludwig made it, too, and threw the ball to Yvonne. Yvonne walked to the foul line, aimed, and *swiiiish,* the ball flew through the hoop. I felt my heart banging wildly against my chest. Yvonne threw me the ball, but I was a little slow. My fingers grazed it, but before I could stop its flight, it was gone, off to the right. I went after it, tripped, and fell.

I was lying flat on my stomach. I could smell the shellac on the gym's wooden floor, feel grainy dust on the palms of my hand. I heard a squeak next to my ear. It was Frau Sander's sneakers.

"You okay?" Frau Sander asked, helping me up and handing me the ball.

I nodded and went to the free-throw line. It was so quiet in the gym, I could practically hear my kneecap rubbing against its cartilage. I aimed. And the bell rang. Class was over. I dropped my arms. Saved by the bell!

Frau Sander blew her whistle and waved us over to the bleachers. "Okay, girls. Over here a sec."

Thirty girls crowded around petite, ponytailed Beate Sander. From afar she looked like one of us, but when you got up close, you could see she's been an adult for a while. But I liked her. I just wish she taught physics instead of physical education.

"We'll be having tryouts again for the girls' basketball team in a few weeks," Frau Sander said. "We need two new players in your age group. Anyone interested?"

Yvonne, Tall Tillie, and a couple of other girls raised their hands. Frau Sander wrote their names down and looked back up. "Anyone else?" she asked.

I looked down, evading her eyes. There was no way I was going to try out for the basketball team and make a stupid fool of myself.

"Well, I see there's going to be stiff competition," Frau Sander said. "But it'll be worth it, girls. Our team's been invited to European playoffs in England, in the spring. So if any of you are—"

I heard no more. Everything around me blanked out. Everything except the word *England*. Had I heard correctly? Playoffs? Playoffs in England? In E-n-g-l-a-n-d?

That was it! My ticket to Buckingham Palace.

I raised my hand. "Excuse me."

"Yes?" said Frau Sander.

"Me, too," I said. "You can sign me up, too."

"For what?" she asked, genuinely confused.

"For the tryouts. I'm trying out for the basketball team."

"You've got to be kidding!" Yvonne said to me. "Are you sure you heard right?"

The locker room was hot from the showers, and smelly from pubescent perspiration and girls' deodorant. I felt a little lightheaded. I looked up and saw Yvonne swing her MCM handbag over her shoulder. I noticed a bunch of girls from gym staring at me, too.

My head was spinning.

"The tryouts are for the basketball team. Not for the National Association of Nerds," Yvonne said.

"I heard," I said. "I'm not deaf." I bent down to tie my shoes.

"You may not be deaf, but you sure are uncoordinated!" Caroline said.

"Tsk, tsk, Caroline," Yvonne said, shaking her head. "You're so unfair to poor Nelly. She has excellent coordination. Look, she can sit and tie her shoelaces at the same time."

The girls' laughter was drowned out by the sound of the bell for the next class. They picked up their things and scrambled away.

Peace.

I closed my eyes and waited for a beautiful starry sky to appear. Then I saw myself rise and float into its deep blackness. I soared higher and higher, on past one diamond of light to another. In the distance, I saw Prince William coming toward me, William in his three-piece, dark blue, pinstriped, cashmere-blend suit. He held out his hand and took me in his arms. As I put my head on his shoulder, my lips grazed the soft fuzz on the nape of his neck. My stomach felt funny. My lips tingled. We danced on and on, past my mother, astonished to see me, a graceful princess, with William, the prince of princes. William spun me around and around, past Yvonne and Caroline and Nicole, all of them clearly envious, on past Pia and Anton, on past the entire student body.

Me, Nelly, William's chosen one.

I opened my eyes.

I'll show them, I thought. I'll show them all.

I stood up. Skinny. Uncoordinated. Knock-kneed. But determined. I had a goal in life. I was going to be a princess. But first, of course, I'd have to learn how to dribble.

I stepped on the footstool and stretched all the way up, up, up. I managed to get ahold of the book I wanted and pull it out and down. *Basketball for Klutzes.* Perfect.

The more I thought about it, the more I knew that getting on the basketball team was exactly what I needed. It would get me to England and give me a fighting chance at attracting William's attention. I wanted it more than anything else in the world. More than Yvonne's super-straight hair. More than the Vixen telescope. But how could I get on the team? Learning how to play basketball seemed as awesome a task as, let's say, jetting to Alpha Centauri.

I stepped off the stool. Leaning against the school library bookshelf, I flipped through the pages of the book.

"You're reading again," a voice said.

Pia Pankewitz. Of course. She was always crawling out of the woodwork.

"I'm surprised to see you here," she went on. "I've noticed that lately you've been reading less than usual."

"Oh?" I said, although I knew she was right. I still carried books around with me wherever I went, but on the bus ride to school, during recess, and sometimes after lunch, I also spent quality time daydreaming instead of reading.

"Well, frankly, I'm surprised to see *you* in the library," I said, using my newly cultivated British accent. I'd practice it with her.

My comment seemed to offend Pia, so I returned to her original question. "I've been preoccupied with something. That's why I've been reading a bit less than usual."

"Well, it must be something terrific, because you were just smiling to yourself."

I blushed.

"It's a boy, isn't it?" she went on.

How did *she* know?

"I figured as much," she said, not even waiting for me to reply. "Who is it? Do I know him?"

I shook my head.

"Oh, come on. Tell me!" she urged.

I merely looked at her.

"Out with it. Who? Arnold Schwarzenegger?"

"Anton Weissenberger? You've got to be kidding!" I said, so loud, in fact, some of the kids sitting at tables looked at us. I lowered my voice. "That's the stupidest thing I ever heard. I already told you I'm not interested in Anton Weissenberger."

"Well, then, if you're really absolutely not interested, then I want to ask you to do me a favor."

I should do Pia Pankewitz a favor?

Before I knew it, Pia and I were sitting in a café, each of us with a strawberry milkshake in front of us. Well, actually, during the ten minutes we'd been there talking, Pia had already finished hers. I'd barely touched mine.

"Let me get this straight," I said. "You're in love with Anton Weissenberger. And you want me to write a letter to him for you so—"

"An *anonymous* letter," Pia interrupted. "It must be anonymous. With beautiful prose. No spelling errors. More words than commas, okay? And then we wait a few days and we see if he knows it's from me. Can you handle it?"

Without even thinking, I knew exactly what I had to do. "All right," I said. "I'll help you out with Schwarzenegger, but you have to help me out, too."

"How?" she asked, narrowing her eyes.

"I want you to practice basketball with me. I need to get on the team."

She stared at me for what seemed like eons. Finally she said, "You? On the basketball team? Why?"

My cheeks burned. Should I or should I not confide in her?

I studied Pia a moment. She had a pretty face— peaches-and-cream complexion, full lips, soft green eyes, long red hair. In her green Scotch plaid kilt and blazer, she looked like she could be the cover girl for a Burberry advertisement. But more important: she didn't look mean, and I was certain she wasn't. Okay, she was a little lamebrained, but I was sure she could keep a secret.

"Prince William lives in England," I finally said.

"Ooooh! So *that's* it!" She looked pretty astonished. "Now I understand. William! Gosh he's cute. The most attractive member of the royal family."

"It doesn't take much to be attractive in that family, but, yes, he *is* handsome."

"So you're aiming to be Queen Nelly?"

"I haven't given marriage much thought yet. I would like to meet the groom first."

Pia laughed. She thought I was joking. And I guess I was. More or less.

She was silent a moment, thinking hard. Finally: "You know, if you want to be the queen, you'll probably have to play cricket and polo, and learn how to ride a horse and speak with a British accent."

"I already speak with an accent," I said, wondering why she hadn't noticed it.

Her face lit up. "So that's it! The whole time I was trying to figure out what's different. I was wondering why you sounded like you had popcorn in your mouth! Wait a second! Are you even allowed to marry him? I mean because you're Jewish."

"Who said I wanted to marry him? But if I did, my mother married a Gentile, didn't she?"

"I mean *him*. Maybe he can't marry *you*."

"Oh. Well, then, he'll have to abdicate," I said.

"Abdicate?"

"You really have to read more English. It means to give up the throne."

I was tired of the direction this conversation was going. I decided to change the subject. And soften my accent a little. "And what if Schwarzenegger doesn't know that the letter's from me—I mean *you*?" I asked.

"Then you write another one," she said eagerly, happy to be talking about Anton again. "And on and on. Eventually he'll know it's you. I mean me. But by then he'll be so charmed by my letters, he'll kiss the ground I walk on."

I was far from convinced. But hey, who was I to argue? "Okay," I said. "I write your letters; you help me with basketball."

"It's a deal."

We shook hands.

"So, now that we're friends, can I borrow your book about black holes?" Pia asked.

"Who says we're friends? We're business partners. And what's with you and black holes?"

Pia shrugged. "Why not?"

My hand dove into my backpack, searching for the book. Out of the corner of my eye, I saw Pia reach over and take my milkshake.

"Hey, that's mine," I said, reaching out for the glass.

"Not anymore, it isn't. You're in training. No sweets."

7 In Training

"No!" Pia shouted as she watched me dribble around her kitchen table.

It was raining, so Pia had transferred our first day of practice indoors.

"How many times do I have to tell you?" she went on. "Dribble with your fingertips, not your palm. It says so right here in your handbook."

I looked down at the ball to see what my hand was doing.

"No!" she said. "It says here not to look down. Look at me when you dribble."

I looked up at Pia and saw her leaning against the refrigerator with my manual. What I didn't see was the vacuum cleaner cord. *Uff!*

It rained on our second day of training, too.

"Let's do some indoor strength training," Pia said. "It says in your book that you have to get into basketball shape. Lie down."

Pia forced me to stretch and squat and twist my body until I collapsed into a heap on her bedroom floor. And then I had to do stomach crunches. Each time I raised my head, I looked into the doleful eyes of a brown colt stuck up on Pia's wall. For days afterward I had nightmares about a ferociously neighing horse.

On our third day of training—what a surprise!— it rained, too. "Then we'll go in the kitchen, where there's linoleum," Pia instructed, "and practice dribbling. You dribble in place and I hold up my hand. You have to tell me how many fingers I'm holding up. This teaches you not to look at the ball."

We did this for a bit with a fair amount of success, until Pia told me to close my eyes and dribble the ball five times. I lost control of the ball, and it plopped right into a bucket of dirty water that Pia's mother had been using to clean the floors, toppling the bucket over. When I lunged for a cloth to sop up the mess, I slipped on the waxed floor. My clothes got soaked, and I had to go home in one of Pia's dresses, three sizes larger than mine.

It was clearly a case of the blind leading the blind, but I kept my side of the bargain and wrote Anton Weissenberger a love letter for Pia: "Hello, Anton, I'm your mystery lady," et cetera.

*   *   *

My parents knew nothing of my future career in basketball. Of course I debated with myself the pros and cons of revealing my athletic ambitions, and actually, one morning, decided to tell my mother. She had once been a cheerleader in junior high school, and I hoped she would be happy to know that I was making an effort to be physical. But when I got to the breakfast table that morning, I lost courage. My parents were not in the best of moods. The night before, they'd come home late from Ari Landau's daughter's wedding, where my father had played klezmer. They'd been fighting and it woke me up. I'd looked at the clock: 2 A.M.

"At least you could have the decency not to do it in front of me!" I'd heard my mother say.

"Lucy, you have an active imagination."

"My imagination isn't nearly as active as your libido," my mother had shouted, slamming the bathroom door.

I closed my eyes and crept under the blanket. "Libido," I thought. "I know that word from somewhere." But I was too tired to think straight, and fell back asleep.

Now, at the breakfast table, we ate in silence, my mother, my father, and I, storm clouds hovering, just waiting for the right moment to rain down on us. Finally, a cloudburst.

"A real Jewish American deli!" my mother said with such a look of disgust, I thought the granola she had just eaten was about to return to her bowl.

"And since when does a 'real Jewish American deli' have a house band?"

"Lucy," my father said, "come on. She can do whatever she pleases."

"Who's she?" I wanted to know.

"And are you going to let her do whatever she pleases?" my mother said.

"Melissa Minsky," my father said to me.

"Your father's new boss," said my mother. "A food specialist—the type that likes to be seen cooking in a Giorgio Armani apron. A German. She went to New York, married an American, and thinks she can come back fifteen years later and open up 'Berlin's first real Jewish American deli.' What crap!"

"I like deli food," I said.

"You don't know what you're talking about," she said. "If it's real Jewish food, everything's served floating in chicken fat or smothered in globs of schmaltz. No one will want to eat it."

"Then I'll be out of a job," my father said. He turned to me. "Frau Minsky wants me to perform once a week at the restaurant and organize her music programs."

"Oh, great! That's terrific," I said. It was. It really was. Where was the problem?

Problems—imaginary and otherwise—continued to pop up. That following Monday marked the end of my Hebrew school career. This time *Basketball for*

Klutzes was my demise. My classmate David was stuttering away, reciting from the Torah, while I was deep into a chapter about free-throwing in my basketball manual, when I suddenly heard my name.

"Yes?" I said, looking up.

"Nelly, you are prepared to be reading to us in Hebrew, too?" Wladimir Kasarow asked. He gestured toward my book. "Which page?"

"In *this* book?" I said, pointing incredulously to the basketball manual opened on my desk. Was he blind, or what?

"Of course! That book!"

He was blind.

"But ..." I stuttered.

"Do as you are being told."

I didn't *want* to be a wiseacre—he simply gave me no other choice.

"Okay," I said to the class, "turn to page fifty-six." I looked down at my book and I saw my 3-D Prince William postcard, which I used as a bookmark, sticking up in the back. William winked at me.

Everyone turned their Torah books to page fifty-six. Agness Sigalova, who sat next to me, looked at my basketball manual, at me, and then heavenward.

" 'The free throw is basketball's most important shot,' " I recited. " 'Remember, you should be in balance after every shot, even when you follow the shot in case it misses and you're in quest of the rebound—' "

The warts on Kasarow's face shook. The hair in his nose stood up on end. His eyes popped out of their sockets, jumped over the rim of his glasses frames, and flew across the room like projectiles, landing in the dollhouse bathtub. Or, at least, that's what it felt like to me when he boomed, "Nelly Edelmeister! I warned you! Take your books and go! You're expelled! Go!"

I slipped my 3-D Prince William postcard into the manual, took my books, and got the hell out of there.

Boy oh boy, was I in big, big trouble.

"Don't have a heart attack, Mom," I said the second my mother walked into the kitchen later that evening, "but Wladimir Kasarow kicked me out of Hebrew school."

She had a heart attack.

Later, after her blood pressure was back to normal and she had been briefed by me in the circumstances surrounding my dismissal, all she could think to ask was, "A *basketball* guide? Why in God's name were you reading a basketball manual?"

"Because."

"Because why?"

My mother's eyebrows creased and I could see her eyes shift into their x-ray vision mode. X-ray vision runs in the maternal side of my family. My mother says I have it, too—I just have to believe in it. And if I do, I'll be able to see through everything. Hearts, brains, even shopping bags.

"Why, Nelly?" my mother asked again, her x-ray eyes piercing my soul. "Why were you reading a basketball manual?"

I decided to come clean. Her x-ray eyes would detect the truth anyway.

"Because I'm learning how to play basketball," I said, "so I can try out for the school's basketball team."

In my whole life I've never seen my mother so surprised. After her initial shock, she managed to ask, "Why? Why basketball?"

"The basketball team's playing in England this year and since *you're* not going to give me money to travel to England, I thought maybe my school will."

She was not at all amused.

"This is what you want?" she asked. "You want to forget all about your bat mitzvah because you have a crush on a prince?"

"All I know is that I don't want to be a hypocrite. That's *your* department."

My mother swallowed hard.

"You're not religious," I said, "so why should I be? The only reason you go to synagogue is to chat up the rabbi or the cantor or Herr Lerner, or anyone else who might be valuable to you."

My mother was horrified. "Do you have any idea what you're talking about?"

"Look, I don't care. I just don't care about being Jewish."

"But basketball?" she asked, focusing her x-ray eyes on me. "You really care about basketball?"

I just stared at her, mustering all the defiance I could. Eventually she got up and left.

Our household was monosyllabic for a couple of days. My parents were still fuming about the deli queen, and mentioning either basketball or the bat mitzvah was strictly taboo. I was a little blue myself, for it seemed I was getting nowhere with basketball. All I had to show for my effort were a couple of black-and-blue marks and sore muscles. One evening, while I was practicing hoops with the makeshift basket above the frame of my door, Risa dropped by with a skirt she had shortened for me. She opened my closet to hang it up, brushing accidentally against my Prince William poster. "Oh, pardon me. I didn't see you," she said to William.

I giggled. Risa was sometimes so funny. And she was a ham, too. When she noticed she had me as her willing audience, she went all out.

"You simply must tell me the name of your tailor!" she said to William. "I am intrigued by your suit." She picked up my magnifying glass from my desk and held it up to the poster like Sherlock Holmes. "Very interesting. Look at that double-stitching. So fancy." Her fingers grazed the poster. "Ooh! A cashmere blend. Very fine. Very fine, indeed."

I threw my pillow at her, and some of the feathers flew out. "Risa! You're making fun of me! Stop it!"

We were both laughing pretty hard. Risa sat down and tried to catch her breath. She patted the bed next to her. "Come sit with me, bubeleh."

Uh-oh. That sounded like she had something on her mind. "I smell a spy," I said, plopping down next to her. "Did my mother send you in here?"

"Absolutely not." She hugged me. "I love you, bubeleh. Like my own granddaughter. And I love your mama, like my own child. And I adore your father."

"Me, too!"

"Shhh! I'm talking." She paused to get back her train of thought. "How many men would let an old lady like me live with them? But your papa, ah, he has a big heart. Sometimes too big," she said, pausing a moment. "But then again, we all have our faults, don't we?" She then said, looking at me with such intense eyes that I wondered if maybe she had x-ray vision, too, "And I want the best for all of you."

"I know," I said, snuggling into her embrace. My nose rubbed against her glass stone. It felt warm.

"Good. Then answer me one question."

I immediately knew something was coming.

"If you never wanted a bat mitzvah," she asked, "why did you go to Hebrew school?"

So there it was. Out in the open. My bat mitzvah. I knew it. "Because of my mother. She wanted me to. So I did."

"Aha!" Risa said.

"What's that supposed to mean? Aha?"

"*Kibbud av va'em*. Respect for parents. A solid base on which to become a good member of the Jewish community."

I was being tricked into something. I was sure of it. Absolutely. But all Risa did was stand up and say, "How about a round of *Doppelkopf*?"

It was a typical early evening at the Golden Residence for the Aged. I was winning our game of *Doppelkopf*; Frau Lewi was feasting on junk food: peanut flips, nachos, and paprika chips; Frau Goldfarb was complaining about Risa's hunched-up posture. "Frau Ginsberg," she said, "you're all slumped."

"Because I don't want anyone looking at my cards," Risa said.

"Uh-uh. I bet you're not taking your calcium pills. That's why your back is like that."

"They give me constipation."

I laughed. I love the way old people have no inhibitions when it comes to talking about their health.

"Well, you look like a pretzel," said Frau Lewi, chasing a handful of nachos down with a couple of gulps of Coke. She looked at the cards on the table and then at Risa. "It's your turn."

"Look at me," said Frau Goldfarb, raising her arm and flexing her muscle, "as strong as an ox and as straight as a rod. You need to build up your bones,

Frau Ginsberg." Her hand started shaking something terrible. I watched it flutter back to the tabletop.

"Bones schmones," said Risa. "They survived worse than hell without calcium." She threw out a nine of clubs.

"That's exactly my point!" said Frau Goldfarb. "Listen, you want to outlive Leni Riefenstahl? Take the calcium."

And that was that.

We finished a round of cards in silence. It was Frau Goldfarb's turn to deal. Frau Lewi turned to me. "I heard you told off that old fart of a Hebrew teacher. Excuse my Yiddish."

"You need him like I need calcium," said Risa.

I had to laugh. That's why I was always visiting the home: those women cracked me up!

"You've got us now, anyway," Frau Lewi added.

My eyes narrowed, smelling something fishy. "You? I've got you?"

"We're going to give the bat mitzvah one more try, bubeleh," said Risa. "If we all work hard, we can pull you through."

"What?"

"Yes," said Frau Goldfarb, who was trying desperately despite the shakes to mix the cards. "Forget Wladimir Kasarow. *We're* your new tutors. What's your Torah portion, *Schätzchen*? What part of the Torah do you have to read?"

I was speechless.

"She reads Parshas Bereishis," said Risa. "Here,

let me help you with those cards, Frau Goldfarb."
She gathered up the cards and started mixing
them.

"Ah! Genesis. The story of Creation. How lucky
you are, Nelly!" said Frau Goldfarb.

"But why, Risa? What do you care if I have a bat
mitzvah or not? What's the use?" I said.

Risa put the cards down, turned to me, and, with
an earnestness that made me sit up straight, said,
"What's the use? This little snotnose asks me what's
the use? Asks me why she should become a member
of the Jewish community? I'll tell you why. Because
it's home. Even if you wander, and most likely you
will, at least you'll always know where home is.
That's why."

How can you say no to that? How can you say
no to someone like Risa? If I'd known, I might
have. But I didn't.

"Okay," I said. "For you. I'll do it for you, Risa."

She shook her head. "Not for me, bubeleh. For
you. But that, of course, you must learn."

It wasn't enough that I had to become a basketball
pro and had to further my knowledge of British
habits, manners, and history. Now I also had three
old ladies *and* my mother on my back about my bat
mitzvah. One evening you could find me in Risa's living room reciting my Torah portion in Hebrew as she
took measurements for my bat mitzvah dress, and the
next day I was out with Pia stubbing my toes trying to

101

play basketball, or visiting with Frau Goldfarb and Frau Lewi.

All in all I have to admit I made much more progress with my Hebrew studies than I did with basketball. Frau Goldfarb and Frau Lewi were pleased. Risa, though, was a hard nut to crack.

"Not bad," she said one day when we were out buying fabric for my dress. Risa was walking from display table to display table, touching, smelling, pulling, stretching material on dozens of fabric bolts while I went through the Creation story. "Not bad, bubeleh. But not good enough. You're getting there. But more important than just memorizing the Hebrew, you should know what the Torah is saying. If you know what it means, one day it may help you to understand life better."

"Oh, Risa!" Sometimes she was really exasperating. "You're talking to a future cosmologist. I can't take the Creation story seriously."

"But you must!" She picked up a bolt of royal blue velvet and held it up to my face. "I like this color for you. What do you say?"

"Everyone knows that the universe began with the big bang. There wasn't a God hanging out with some angels on cloud nine who said, 'and then there was light,' and six days later he decided to create man." The royal blue velvet had a lustrous sheen. I felt compelled to reach out and touch it. It was soft and cuddly, like my childhood velveteen bunny. "It's nice," I said.

"Nelly." Risa's eyes were earnest. "The Creation story doesn't want to explain *how* the world was made. The Torah isn't a science textbook or a lesson in evolution. The story just wants us to feel the poetry, the wonder, the wonder at how life began. And it tells us that *one* force created the earth and that we have to help that force care for it. Now, I call the force God. You can call it whatever you like."

"Physics. The force is called physics," I said. "Should we get the blue velvet?"

The following morning my father and I were sitting peacefully eating breakfast when the kitchen door suddenly swung open and in stampeded my mother. She slammed the door behind her—*bang!*—threw a newspaper down on the table—*tchonk!*—and snorted a big "Ha!"

We looked up from our granola.

"She's some opportunist, that Melissa Minsky!" my mother said. She looked at my father. "What time are you meeting her?"

"At eight, Lucy," he said wearily—as if he had already told her that at least a hundred times.

"Well, you can tell her I think this interview in the paper is a bunch of baloney." She sat down and started attacking her toast.

"I won't tell her that. I want that job."

"She's going to be serving Jewish food at that restaurant as if it were nouvelle cuisine," she said to me, hoping to win me over as an ally. "She'll probably call her house specialty"—my mother put on a French accent here—" 'tenderlee shopped feesh balls avec orse radeesh and a carrott garneesh,' instead of plain old stupid gefilte fish! She's just capitalizing on the Jewish thing if you ask me."

"It's a job for me, Lucy," my father said.

"Thank God for small miracles." My mother turned to me. "It says here she has a five-year-old son. Maximilian's his name. Maybe he needs a babysitter."

"Don't I have enough to do already, Mom?"

"It's not a bad idea, princess," my father said. He winked at me. "You could start saving for that telescope."

"Or for a new basketball," my mother said.

Was she trying to be funny or just sarcastic?

"So it's settled?" my mother said. She looked at me, then at my father, and then back at me. "Good! So why don't you go with your father to the Minskys' this evening. When was that again? At eight?" My mother smiled sweetly at my father. It was too sweet. Like Manischewitz wine.

I was not thrilled with the idea of baby-sitting, but if it kept my mother off my back I was willing to try it out. My plan was to play a little with the child while my father and Melissa Minsky talked business. If the boy and I got along, I'd ask Melissa if she needed a babysitter.

Believe me, I had no idea what I was getting into.

The most stunning human being I have ever seen answered the door. It was Melissa Minsky.

My mother has this photography book with pictures of international film stars from the fifties and sixties—each one more beautiful than the next. Well, Melissa Minsky could have been in it, too. I swear, she was a real knockout, a cross between Marilyn Monroe and Doris Day, but with long hair.

Melissa Minsky didn't know that my father was going to bring me along to the meeting, so she looked a little surprised to see me. She ushered us into the living room. "I had no idea you had a grown daughter," she said to my father.

"Neither did I," he said.

I gave him a stage punch. "Papa!"

My father pretended to buckle up from the pain. "Aagghh!"

Melissa's living room was out of the pages of *House Beautiful*. I discreetly looked at the soles of my shoes to make sure I hadn't brought any dog poop into the house with me.

"Make yourselves comfortable," Melissa said. She pointed to a tray of beautifully sculptured canapés. It was displayed on a slab of glass that doubled as a coffee table. "Help yourselves. Can I get you grown-ups something to drink?"

"Yes," I said. "I'll have a double martini, dry, on the rocks."

They laughed, but frankly, I really could have used a stiff drink. That's how anxious I was about the prospect of baby-sitting.

"I'll just go and play with Maximilian, if you don't mind," I said.

"With Max?" Melissa said. "You want to *play* with Max?"

"Oh, I'm sorry. Is he already asleep?"

"No, no, of course not. He's in his room," she said, pointing vaguely in the direction of the hall.

As I walked toward Max's room, I heard Melissa say to my father, "I suppose she'll be all right."

"She's never baby-sat before," said my father, munching one of the finger food art pieces. "Mmm. These are fabulous."

"Baby-sat?" said Melissa.

There was a sign on Max's door that said KEEP OUT! I knocked anyway.

No answer.

I knocked again. "Maximilian?" I waited a moment, then opened the door and closed it behind me.

I was in darkness, but on the right-hand wall there was a door leading to another room, and I saw some light streaming through on the bottom. "Maximilian?" I called out. "Hello? Max? Where are you?" I walked across the room to the other door, knocked, and then peeked in.

This room, too, was in total darkness, save for a small beam of light directed at a bed, on which I saw a ghost, no, an ailing and deathly pale tuberculosis patient, no, a healthy vampire, reclining, reading a large, black, linen-bound book with gold lettering. He was pretty big for a five-year-old—almost as tall as my father. He, it, was dressed in black from shoulder to toe. His face was white, literally as white as chalk. Black, spiderweb-like designs were painted on his cheeks. Dark goo that had dried and stiffened outlined his hairline and his eyebrows. His hair was stiff, too, black and spiky. His shoes were scuffed, black, and spiked. When he talked, I was relieved to see that his teeth were not fangs.

"Who the hell are you?" he said in perfect American-accented English.

I'm usually not at a loss for words. But I was now.

"And what the hell are you doing in here?" he went on, sitting up. His book fell down, but he paid no attention. I saw the gold lettering shimmer. "Can't you read?" he said, pointing to the door. "It says 'Keep Out.'"

"I was looking for Max."

"Max? What for?"

"I thought I'd play with him. Baby-sit."

The bête noire stood up. Yes, he was almost as tall as my father. He took a step toward me. "Baby-sit? You've got to be kidding."

And then, of course, I understood. "Omigod," I said. "Are *you* Maximilian?"

"No one's allowed in here. Ever. Get out. Now!"

*   *   *

"Papa!" I said, barging back into the Minskys' living room. "Papa!"

I was infuriated, embarrassed, confused.

"Oh, dear," Melissa said, as she hastily rose. "I expected something like this."

"That boy does not need a babysitter!" I said.

"You're quite right," said Melissa. "He doesn't."

"If you ask me, he needs a psychiatrist!"

My father shook his head. "Nelly!"

"No, Benny, she's right. He already has one."

"At five?" said my father.

"Five? Oh! So that's it!" said Melissa. "You read that story in the paper. It was a typo. He's not five. He's fifteen."

"Fifteen?" said my father.

"But he acts like he's three," I said.

My father wagged his finger at me. "Nelly!"

"No, Benny," Melissa said, putting her hand on his arm. "She's right. He does act like he's three sometimes."

Since when did she call my father Benny? That was the second time. And since when did she put her hand on his arm?

"Mom!" said a voice.

It was Count Dracula Jr. We watched him swing a long velvet black cape over his shoulders. My father was so taken by the entrance, he whistled.

"Max, I'd like you to meet Benny Edelmeister," Melissa said. "I believe you already met his daughter, Nelly Sue?"

Drac Jr. ignored the courtesy of the introduction. "You sent her in to *baby-sit* for me?"

"Oh, Max, don't be silly. Of course not. It was a mistake."

"I'm out of here," he said, walking away. He stopped at the door, turned back, and pointed a finger at me. "And you! You stay out of my room! You hear?" And then he disappeared, slamming the door behind him.

"Max'll be starting at the Twain School at the end of the week," Melissa said. "We've been here a couple of weeks, but I thought I'd give him some time to get used to Berlin first. Now I think Berlin has to get used to him."

"Does he go out like that?" my father asked.

"I'm afraid so. Yesterday, at least, he did. He's at a difficult stage." She shook her head and frowned.

Difficult? Maximilian Minsky was not what I'd call difficult. He was demented. But I left the remark unchallenged. I was too busy taking in Melissa. She was fascinating to look at. Her movements were so graceful that when she walked, she gave the impression of floating underwater. She was the exact opposite of my mother. My mother entered a room like a raging typhoon; Melissa, like a gentle May breeze in an apple orchard. My mother clunked in her shoes like a Dutch milkmaid in clogs. Melissa's toes barely touched earth. My mother wore loose-fitting, bulky, black wools. Melissa wore tight-fitting, white silk chiffon that fell in soft ripples. My mother's head was covered with short, frizzy, brunette-turning-gray stubble. Melissa had luxuriously long blond tresses that fell in soft waves over her shoulders.

"Too bad your first impression of Max was so negative," Melissa was saying to me. "It would be good for him to have someone from his school to talk to in German."

I smiled politely. No way was I going to talk to Maximilian Minsky again. In *any* language.

We were downstairs in the area that would soon be Minsky's, Berlin's First Real Jewish American Deli. I don't care what my mother says, I like deli food and Jewish cooking. There's a great deli around the corner from my uncle Bruce and aunt Debbie's in Manhattan. Epstein's. I used to have a frank with sauerkraut, homemade French fries, and a celery soda there every day after the planetarium. And the best meal I ever had was at Aunt Debbie's grandmother Bella Lustig's house. She was eighty-five and she cooked *kasha varnishkes* for eight people. Those are bow-tie noodles fried with buck-wheat and onions and schmaltz. It was to die for. Wasn't it just like my mother to make a big deal about getting the recipe from Bella, and then mis-placing it? Maybe Melissa Minsky will serve *kasha varnishkes* in her restaurant.

So yes, I thought it was about time there was a restaurant like Minsky's in Berlin. There should be more. Frankly, I didn't see why my mother was so upset about a deli opening here. She's the one who's always saying there should be more of everything Jewish in Berlin. Restaurants. Writers. Dentists. And they should let everyone know that they're Jewish. "How are Jews ever going to be considered normal here if they're not a part of everyday life?" she's always saying. "The day I see a Jewish German sitcom on German television, I'll know life is back to normal."

I keep on telling my mother *she* should write the sitcom if she wants it so much—help speed up the process. But then she says, "I want to write my own book. Besides, it's up to the Germans to write a German Jewish sitcom, not me."

So? So why's she unhappy that they interviewed Melissa in the paper? Isn't it better to read an interview with a beautiful German Jew (i.e., Melissa Minsky) who returns to Berlin from New York to cook great food, than about the number of graves that have been defaced in the past six months in Jewish cemeteries? Not that we shouldn't read about the graves. But wouldn't it be better if we could read *more* about restaurants and beautiful women and just *normal* Jewish things, normal Jews doing normal things like normal everybody elses?

I turned to Melissa Minsky. "Will you be serving *kasha varnishkes*?" I asked.

"Kasha varnishkes?" Melissa's face brightened. I could tell she really liked food. "My poor grand-

mother would turn in her grave if she thought I weren't. Of course I'm serving them!"

I looked at the kitchen. It was hard to imagine anyone cooking here. There wasn't much to see yet except lots of space, buckets of paint, tools, a couple of tables and chairs, and a bunch of holes in the walls. We walked into the future dining hall. "This is where we'll put the stage," Melissa said, walking to a corner. She wore high, spiky heels—just like Frau Goldfarb. Although I must say they looked far better on Melissa. She turned to my father. "I like your dinner show idea, Benny. You and your band can play once a week. And on a couple of the other nights, you can book guest acts, standup comics, instrumentalists. A lot of Americans. The Germans get a kick out of Americans."

"He knows," I said. "He's married to one."

Melissa flushed. "I was married to one, too." She turned to my father, but he looked away and Melissa turned to the window.

The entire back wall was a window front, about eight meters across. Outside, in the building's inner courtyard, we saw Maximilian moving about. It was hard to see what he was doing because it was dark outside and there was a glare in the window. Melissa looked at him a moment and then came to me. "Nelly, how would you like to tutor Max in German? I suspect he knows more than he's letting on. When he was a child, I spoke to him in German."

Tutor Max? Oh, Barbie's dream come true.

112

"Thank you for offering," I said, "but frankly I don't think we'd get along."

"His bark is much worse than his bite. He's only trying to provoke me." She walked up to the window and peered out.

I looked at my father and shook my head vigorously. He nodded. He knew I would never do anything with that vampire out there.

Suddenly, I heard a familiar sound coming from outside: a dribbling basketball. I walked up to the window and held my face against the glass. Melissa was standing beside me. She smelled like the ground floor of Bloomingdale's in New York, like the cosmetic and perfume department. Exciting and expensive. Her perfume was so pungent it stung my nose.

"He was assistant captain of his school's basketball team," Melissa said wistfully. "He's a wonderful player."

And then I saw him. He looked like a huge bat. His cape was fluttering in the breeze and when he ran, dribbling the ball, playing an invisible foe, he really seemed to be flying. He raced across the courtyard, stopped short, jumped, and shot the ball. There was a basket set up and the ball flew through it and then bounced back into Max's hands. He took another jump shot. And scored. And then another hoop. And another.

I could scarcely breathe. "Okay," I said to Melissa, barely containing my excitement. "Okay, I'll do it."

Melissa looked at me, puzzled. My father took a step toward me, a question mark in his eyes.

"Do what?" Melissa asked.

"I'll do it," I repeated. "I'll start tutoring Max tomorrow."

EDUCATING MAX

The door slammed and Max stomped across the living-room floor. He stopped in front of me, his legs spread apart. His words came like bullets. "I want you to know I hate German. I hate Berlin. I hate this house. I hate this room." He plunged down into the armchair, chucking *German for Foreigners* onto the coffee table. "And I hate this book!" I watched the book slide across the glass as if on ice. It fell onto the floor next to me. I reached down to pick it up.

"Don't!" Max commanded.

I sat back up.

Max glared at me.

I glared at Max.

"And the table, too!" he added. "I hate it!"

We stared at each other for another second or

two. Besides the whiteface with the spiderweb design, he now had a ring hanging from his nose.

"I thought the first few days we should work on conversational skills," I said in a teacherly voice. "Phrases you need every day. Please open your book to page six."

Max looked at me incredulously. I noticed that he had blue eyes.

I waited for him to pick up his book.

Eventually he did.

We plodded through the first chapter. Word by word. Sentence by sentence. It took a while.

Outside, in the kitchen, I heard Melissa and my father laugh.

"Know what they're doing in there?" Max said.

"What do you mean?"

Max smirked. Then he grabbed a bottle of soda that was on the end table, raised it to his mouth, and gulped down what must have been at least half a liter. Then he burped. Twice.

Really: I decidedly did not like him. But I needed him. He was my ticket to Buckingham Palace. I had to figure him out so I could get him to coach me. I sighed and looked at the clock. Another half hour to go.

"Okay, let's work through the text one more time. *Guten-Tag*," I said, reading from my book, starting again with the hellos, how-are-yous, and my-name-is-such-and-such-what's-yours?

"*Guten-Tag*," Max answered sullenly. He grabbed

a piece of cake from the tray on the table and stuffed it into his mouth. "Good day," he said, opening his mouth so wide I could see his half-masticated food.

"*Ich-heiße-Nelly. Wie-heißt-du?*" I went on, making a face—less at his manners than at the silliness of telling him my name and asking him his.

"*Ich-heiße-Max.*" Some crumbs were hanging from his mouth. He wiped them off with his shirt sleeve.

"*Wie-geht-es-dir-Max?*"

He looked at me vacantly. Had he forgotten that it translated to "How are you?" or did he simply not want to answer?

"*Wie-geht-es-dir-Max?*" I repeated.

"*Mir-geht-es ... geht-es...?*"

"*Gut,*" I said. "*Mir-geht-es-gut.*"

"Good? How the hell do *you* know how I feel?" Max said, jumping up from the sofa and leaning over me menacingly. "What gives you the right to suggest that I'm feeling good?" He stared at me belligerently, daring me to answer.

Who did he think he was? No one talked to me like that. No one, that is, except my mother.

I stood up, too. I wouldn't take treatment like that sitting down. "Well, excuse me for being so presumptuous as to think you might be feeling fine."

"Well, I'm not! I'm not feeling fine! Okay?"

"Thanks for telling me. I wouldn't have known otherwise."

117

I picked up my backpack and turned toward the door. "Class is dismissed."

"I think his hair may be blond," I said to Pia, describing my *enfant terrible* Max, "but you can't tell because he puts this colored stuff in it. First it was pitch-black and then yesterday it was blue."

"And his bod?"

"His bod? You mean his physique?"

"Physique?" She shrugged her shoulders. "I guess so."

I tried to visualize Max. "Well, he's a bit shorter than my father, but not much. And he wears his pants—they're leather—very tight, so his shirttails don't slip out like my father's do."

Pia and I were sitting in the school cafeteria eating lunch. Pia took a sip of her chocolate milk and gestured that I should continue.

"And he's pretty thin," I said. "Thinner, let's say, than Anton Weissenberger, and not nearly as wide, but also well built. I mean, he's not skin and bones." An image of Max's lower arm popped into my head. He was wearing a black shirt with its sleeves rolled up just below his elbow. I could see dark blond hair on his lower arms. And when he leaned back in his armchair and stretched, I saw muscles.

"And?" Pia said.

"And what?"

"And what else?"

"He's bestial," I said. "A real pig. He's impolite. Unrefined. A slob."

"It sounds like you really like him."

I rolled my eyes.

"Well, you better watch out—he sounds weird," Pia said.

"Watch out? I'm not afraid of that creep. It's all show, anyway. His mother says he's only doing it to provoke her. You should see *her*. She's like a model."

"Provoke?"

"He's doing it to needle her."

Pia nodded. Augh. I should give her a reading list. She really had to improve her vocabulary.

"I think I'm going to quit tutoring," I said.

"I wouldn't if I were you," Pia said. "You may never have the opportunity again to work with an ex-assistant captain of an American high school basketball team."

"I haven't even asked him yet. He never gives me the chance."

"Well, you better hurry up and ask. The tryouts are in two weeks."

"But I don't think he'll listen."

"Why don't you offer him something in return? It worked with us."

"But what? What should I offer?"

"You're the one with the brain, Nelly. Figure it out."

*　　*　　*

The next day Max and I were practicing the articles *der, die,* and *das,* never easy for Anglo-Saxons. I could sympathize. In German there is little rhyme or reason as to what's masculine, feminine, or neutral. I was standing in the middle of the Minskys' living room pointing to things, and Max had to say what the object was in German using the proper article. He was actually doing a good job. He was testing himself, I think, and getting quite a kick out of it. Of course he was yawning all over the place as if he were suffering from the worse case of ennui, but it was my first inkling that he wasn't quite as thickheaded as he would like me to think. I pointed to the wall.

"*Die Wand,*" Max said.

I went to the window.

"*Das Fenster.*"

I put my hand on the sofa. It was very soft. And pure white. I didn't really enjoy sitting on it. I was afraid I'd get it dirty. What if the mustard from my sandwich got on it? What if I spilled orange soda? Or accidentally marked it with ink?

"*Das Sofa,*" Max said. "*Das scheiße Sofa.*"

I looked at him.

"*Scheiße,*" he said. "Shit! It's the first word you learn here. It's all over the street." He laughed obnoxiously.

"Well, I would drop the second *e* from *Scheiße* when you use it to build a compound noun," I suggested.

I went on to the next word, pointing to the table.

"*Der Scheißtisch,*" Maximilian said, omitting, correctly, the second *e*.

Clearly he was a quick learner. I tried not to smile. Leaning against the wall, I wondered what to point to next.

"*Der Mund,*" Maximilian said. "Or *die Lippen.*"

Mouth? Lips? I wondered a moment what he could mean, and then realized I had my finger on my mouth. I dropped my hand.

"*Die Busen,*" Max said.

A bosom? What bosom? I looked down. My hand was on my chest. I dropped my hands to my side and cleared my throat. This was getting a little uncomfortable. "*Die Busen* is incorrect," I said.

"Oh? You don't have them yet?"

I felt my cheeks turn crimson. "*Busen* is not feminine. It's masculine. *Der.* And it's singular. *Der Busen.*"

Max's big blue eyes widened. "You only have one breast? And it's masculine?"

"If you want something feminine, use *Brust. Die Brust.*"

"And how many of *them* do you have?"

Max was staring at me. I felt my almost nonexistent breasts tingle. I didn't know what to do with my hands, my body, my eyes. I sat down and grabbed a sandwich from a tray on the table. "Your mother's a great cook," I said.

"I wonder what she and your father are stirring up right now?"

I looked toward the kitchen. It was very quiet in there. Almost too quiet.

Max burst out laughing. I was confused about why, but was aware that things were getting out of hand. I needed to take control. My hand dove into my backpack. Pretending to look for a pen, I pulled *Basketball for Klutzes* out of my backpack, hoping it would catch Max's attention. And it did. He lunged for it like a pit bull terrier for the jugular. But uh-oh, my 3-D Prince William bookmark accidentally fell out.

"A picture of your boyfriend?" Max said, grinning stupidly.

I felt my cheeks burn. This was not what I had planned on. I'd sidetrack him for a few minutes and then weave my way back to basketball. "Why don't we turn now to page twenty-six in our textbook and practice the 'This is ...' construction," I said. "Repeat after me. *Dies ist—*"

"I'm sick of this bullshit!" Max said, popping up from the sofa. "Look, let me level with you, kiddo. The only reason I'm doing this is because my mother promised me a trip to New York for Christmas if I apply myself."

"Then let me level with you, too," I said, although I wondered if you can really level with someone who's wearing a ring through his nose and a chip on his shoulder. "The only reason I'm doing this is because I was hoping you'd teach me how to play basketball."

"Excuse me?" he said.

I think he really thought he hadn't heard correctly.

"I was hoping you'd teach me how to play basketball," I repeated, enunciating carefully. "And if you agree to help me, I'm willing to do something for you in exchange. Just tell me what you want."

"What I want?"

"Yes. We could make a deal. Maybe there's something that you really need. Is there?"

"Something I want?" he asked. "Something I need?"

"Yes."

Max sat up straighter. His eyes suddenly had a glint in them. "Why do you want to play basketball?" he asked.

My first reaction was to tell him the truth—not all of it, of course, but just the right amount to make sense. "The girls' basketball team in school is going to England and I want to go with them. I need to learn how to play basketball."

"You want to learn basketball so you can go to England?" He sounded incredulous. Uh-oh. Maybe I had said too much already.

"Yes, I want to go to England."

"Why?"

Why was he putting me through the grinder like this? "Because," I said.

I hate my cheeks. They always blush at the wrong time. Maybe I should wear whiteface like

Maximilian; then no one would see what color my cheeks were.

I watched Max watch my cheeks turn crimson.

"You want to go to England 'because'?" he said. "Because why?"

And then, at once, I knew that the kid was no slouch.

"Because of Prince William?" he asked.

"Don't be silly," I barely heard myself say, appalled that he had figured me out so fast. I flushed. And my heart raced ahead. It was beating at maximum speed, as if I had just jogged a forty-two-kilometer marathon in less than an hour.

"All right," he said, leaning back. "I know what I want in exchange for helping you."

I had a knot in my throat. I swallowed it down. "And?"

"I want sex," Max said.

"Sex?"

"Yeah, sex."

I should give *him* sex?

I burst out laughing.

Max shot up. "You think that's funny? Well, let me tell you what's *really* hilarious. That you want to go to England. That a little pip-squeak like you wants to play basketball so you can go visit a prince."

I couldn't listen anymore.

"Papa!" I called out. "Papa! Where are you?"

Where was my father? In the back of the apartment? In the bathroom? In the kitchen? "Papa!"

124

I burst into the kitchen. Melissa whipped around, flustered, as if I'd scared her. She was standing next to the open pantry door, her hair in disarray. Her blouse had slipped out of her pants. My father was in the pantry with his back to me. What in the world was he doing in there?

"Papa!" I said, taking another step.

It took him a moment or two, but finally he turned around. "Princess," he said, "what's wrong?" His hair was all mussed up. His shirt had slipped out of his pants, too, but that, of course, was normal for him. "Here's the … uh … wheat germ," he said to Melissa, handing her a jar.

"Can we go?" I said to my father. "Max and I are finished."

My father and I walked home in silence. It smelled like fall. The trees were already losing their leaves. I liked to wade in the fallen leaves, in the sea of orange and red and yellow leaves that line Berlin's side streets in the fall. I liked to scrunch through them and listen to them crackling. Fiona and I used to do it a lot that time of year. But that night it was drizzling, and the foliage was squishy, soft, boring.

"Papa," I said, "do you know anything about basketball?"

"Next to nothing, princess. How about Max?"

"He's a maniac! It's hard to believe he's Melissa's son."

We passed the old gas station where the neighborhood street kids were still hanging out. I looked to see if the Poet was around, but he wasn't.

"They'll be gone soon," my father said to me. "It's getting cold out."

The street kids looked up at us. "Gotta mark?" one of them asked.

We walked by. My father protectively put his arm around me.

"They won't bother us," I said. "They're harmless."

"Just the same."

Melissa and Max were on my mind. It really *was* hard to believe they were mother and son. They were exact opposites: good and bad, white and black, beauty and the beast.

"What do the two of you do all the time when I'm with Max?" I asked.

My father stared at me. "What do you mean?" His voice had a defensive edge to it.

"Nothing. Just what I said. What do you do?"

"We talk."

"About what?"

"About what?" My father just looked at me—as if he expected *me* to answer.

"Music?" I asked.

His face lit up. "Yes, of course. We talk about music. Of course."

We turned the corner to our house.

* * *

"What was so important that you forgot about our meeting?" my mother said to my father, looking up from her book. "We were going to talk about catering for the bat mitzvah."

"Oh, no," my father said. "I forgot. I really forgot."

And he had. I could tell.

We had just gotten home and were standing in the doorway to my mother's home office. My father was on his way to his studio in the back of the apartment, and I was about to tidy myself up for a meeting with Risa. Some newspapers and a stack of *New Yorker*s, my mother's favorite magazine, were strewn across her desk. The floor was cluttered with travel brochures: *USA, American Cities, New York,* and *New England.* My mother wanted to take me with her to New York for Christmas, and then to Vermont to ski. Me on skis—ha! But now, because of her job situation, we couldn't go anyway.

My mother threw her book down. "Oh, Benny!" she said, thoroughly exasperated. "How could you forget?"

"Sorry," I heard my father say as I dropped my backpack off in my room. I tiptoed back to the door to eavesdrop.

"Sorry, honey," my father said. "I waited to take Nelly home." There was a pause, and then, "Anything interesting in the papers?"

"I suppose, if you're straight out of school, have a doctorate and a thirty-six-inch bust. But there's not much for a flat-chested forty-seven-year-old with a pot belly."

I wondered sometimes about that self-mocking tone of hers. Sometimes I couldn't tell if it was a strong point or one of her weaknesses.

"You know, Nelly is perfectly capable of walking home by herself," my mother said.

She was right, of course. But then again, I *liked* my father's company. And he mine. Why shouldn't he walk me home?

"What do you and that woman do all the time while you're waiting for Nelly?" she asked.

I have to admit I was pretty amazed that my mother asked my father the very same question I had. Sometimes I'm surprised at how similar we are.

"We talk, Lucy," my father said.

"Oh? And about what?"

This time his answer came quickly. "Music," he said. "We talk about music."

I don't think my mother said anything after that. At least I didn't hear anything.

I wanted to freshen myself up before meeting Risa. While washing my hands and my face, I remembered how Max had embarrassed me in his living room before, how he had made me feel so self-conscious about my body. And what exactly did he mean when he said "sex"? I should have asked him to be more explicit.

I turned sideways and looked in the mirror.

I could definitely see the shape of a bust. I cupped my breasts and pressed a bit. They felt soft, like two tiny pillows. Okay, they might not have been nearly as visible as Yvonne's, but, hey, they were there and, if need be, could even be seen with the naked eye.

I bent down and pulled out a vanity case from the back of the cabinet. My mother had given it to me as a holiday present, but I barely used it. I found a soft glossy lipstick—Rosy Rosa was the name of it—put it on, blotted my lips like my mother did, and checked myself out in the mirror.

Not bad. Not bad at all.

I wet my lips with my tongue and tasted the lipstick. It was sweet, like raspberry.

I put my right hand on my right hip and swung my hips. I pretended to smoke.

"Nelly," I heard Risa call. "It's getting late."

I wiped off the lipstick.

I was standing on a chair, wrapped in soft folds of blue velvet from my waist to my ankles. The skirt portion of my bat mitzvah dress was almost finished, but Risa hadn't figured the bodice out yet. I looked in the mirror. The blue was right for me. I could tell. We had chosen well.

Risa was standing next to me, pinning the hem. She looked into the mirror and said to my reflection, "So what else is the Creation story about?"

I looked at her in the mirror and made a face.

Reflected behind us was Risa's room, her antiques,

her framed photographs, her sewing machine, her dressmaker's dummy, her Biedermeier furniture. All the way in the back of the mirror was an open door that led to her bedroom and to a bathroom that she and I shared.

"Maybe it should be a little shorter," I said, referring to the hem.

"Bubeleh, you're going to your bat mitzvah, not to a discotheque."

"I know. But…" my voice trailed off. I was fascinated by our image in the mirror. When Risa stood at a certain angle, the glass stone around her neck reflected the light in such a way, it appeared as if sparks were flying out of her chest.

"And?" Risa said.

"And what?"

"The Creation story! If you want to read from the Torah, you have to know what your portion is about. It's not right just to memorize the Hebrew."

"The other kids don't have to interpret."

"I don't care. You are you. I am your tutor. And I say, interpret. Again, what else is the Creation story about?"

"We also learn that Adam and Eve are banned from the Garden of Eden," I said, watching Risa pin my skirt. "Adam and Eve misinterpreted God's commands and that's why he expelled them. This teaches us to watch out about what we say and to take responsibility for our mistakes. If they hadn't blamed each other for eating the apple, or blamed

the snake, or God, God may have thought twice
about throwing them out. And the story of Cain
and Abel teaches us—"

"Come down from the chair, please, so I can
drape this," Risa said.

I jumped down from the chair, and Risa began
working on my bodice. It looked like she was making me long sleeves.

"I don't think I want long sleeves."

Risa's eyes narrowed. We were standing beside
each other. She was small and sturdy, neither thin
nor chubby. I bet when she was younger, she was
what people called a "handsome" woman.

"You don't want long sleeves?" Risa asked.

"No, I want short sleeves."

"In a house of worship?"

"Or sleeveless," I added. "Or maybe even off-
the-shoulder." I draped the material so I could see
my shoulders.

"It's a synagogue. Not a sauna!"

"It's for the reception, not the service. I just want
to see what it looks like."

Risa begrudgingly helped me drape the material
to make an off-the-shoulder effect. I studied myself in the mirror. If I had blond hair and were
older and had more of a bosom, I could possibly
pass for Anita Ekberg in my father's favorite
movie, *La Dolce Vita*—the scene when she's
standing in front of a fountain and she flings her
head back.

Risa pulled my braid. "And what are we going to do with this?"

"My mother said when she was my age she ironed out the frizz."

"Iron! Bubeleh, you have beautiful hair!"

I rolled my eyes.

"Okay, you have ugly hair. So tell me about Cain and Abel instead."

"The story of Cain and Abel teaches us that we're responsible for each other."

"Good," she said. "For a start."

"You really think so?" I asked, looking in the mirror, appraising my dress.

"I loved the book," Pia said, handing me back *Black Holes, White Dwarves, Smart Kids*.

We were out in the schoolyard during recess. It was especially crowded and loud because it was a sunny day. I remember that specifically, for there aren't very many nice sunny days in Berlin during the autumn. When there is one, it sticks in your mind.

"I'm glad you liked the book," I said to Pia. "It wasn't too hard for you?"

"What? The book?" She shrugged. "Well ... I don't know..."

It probably *was* too hard for her, but she was too embarrassed to say so. I quickly changed the subject. "He wants sex," I said.

"Who? What? Where?" she asked, coming to life.

"Max."

Her eyes widened. "He'll teach you basketball if you put out? How exciting!"

"Pia!" I said, giggling. "That's crazy. I wouldn't know what to do."

"So get a book. *Sex for Klutzes* or something. Did he say what kind of sex? How far he wanted to go?"

I couldn't stop giggling. "No. I left the room before he could be explicit."

"Well," she said, "I'd think twice about saying no. It's a great opportunity. And just think: if you ever *do* meet Prince William, you'd know exactly what to do. You'd already be experienced."

"I never thought of it that way." She had something there. She really did. "Okay, I'll think about it," I said, reaching into the side pocket of my backpack and pulling out the letter I had written to Anton for her. It was the second one. We huddled together so no one would see it.

" 'Dear Anton,' " Pia read softly. " 'It's me again, your mystery lady. Whenever I see you, my li—'? What's this word? *Li*—?" Pia looked up at me, knitting her brows.

"Libido. Your sex drive."

"Oh," she said after a moment. "My sex drive. Of course." She smiled as if she'd known it all along, looked down at the letter, but then looked back up. "You're wearing lipstick!"

My cheeks stung. Did she have to say it so loud?

And it was none of her business anyway. "It's medicated lip gloss," I said. "My lips are chapped."

Pia scrutinized my lips. "Really? They don't look it."

"That's because it already helped."

"Oh." She seemed satisfied and went back to the letter. "'I especially enjoy watching you at soccer, the way your glu-te ... glu-te-us—'" She looked at me again.

"Your gluteus muscles," I said. "Those are the muscles in your butt."

She read the sentence again. "'I especially enjoy watching you at soccer, the way your gluteus muscles ripple in the stark sunlight.'" Pia giggled. "I never watched him play soccer *that* closely, have you?"

"It was an e-mail I wrote to Prince William."

Suddenly we realized that we were the only sound in the whole schoolyard. Everyone else had stopped talking, breathing, moving. We heard nothing but a bunch of kindergarten kids in their classroom singing "Old MacDonald."

I looked up.

And I saw a black figure approaching us, a cross between Batman and Darth Vader.

It was Maximilian, of course, decked out in all his glory.

"Oh, my God!" Pia whispered. "Is that him? Christ. You want to have sex with *that*?"

"I never said I wanted to have sex!"

134

The other kids stood there, mesmerized, baffled, full of wonder. We have a lot of weird kids in the school, but this was too much of a provocation. Something had to go: the makeup for sure, the spider-web on his cheeks, the hair goo. They'd let him wear leather, and his boots, and the cape, I supposed. They might even let him keep his hair stuck up like a grass-green porcupine, but what about the ring in his nose?

"I can't believe he came to school like that," I said, watching Max come closer.

Oh, no! Was he walking toward me? To *me*? I looked heavenward. "Oh, God, I promise to study for my bat mitzvah every single day if you keep him away from me. Please, God!"

"I don't think God's listening," Pia said, watching Max approach.

"I'm out of here," I said, gathering my things to make an escape.

But I was too late.

"Hey, Nelly! Where are you going so fast?" I heard Max say. "Wait a second!"

What was I to do? The whole school was looking at me! I turned around and stood face to face with the most obnoxious human being I have ever encountered in my life.

"At least you can introduce me to your friends," he said with a wild smirk on his face.

Did he really think people wanted to make his acquaintance, I was thinking as I was suddenly shoved aside. It was Yvonne.

"Hi," Yvonne said to Max, swinging her hips. "*I'm* one of Nelly's friends. One of her very best. Yvonne. Yvonne Cohen." She gave Max a smile to die for. The little slut. And he reciprocated.

It was no use. I was getting nowhere with that boy. We'd probably never make a deal with basketball, so what did I care if he learned German? And it's not as if the ten marks per hour that I was earning were getting me any closer to my telescope. Nickel and diming my way to a seven-hundred-mark Vixen—even if my mother would contribute half— was not my favorite pastime. Forget it! I was quitting. That afternoon.

But Max wasn't home when I got there, and Melissa had one foot out the door. "I've got an appointment, sugar," she said. "Max should be here any minute. There's some food on the kitchen table. Make yourself at home." And she was gone, leaving a trail of perfume behind her. I stood dazed a minute or two, just breathing it in, letting the sweet mist fill my lungs, settle on my hair and clothes. Eventually, though, I went into the living room and waited.

And waited.

I was bored. I got something to nibble on in the kitchen and poured myself a drink. I walked idly through the apartment, past Max's room with the KEEP OUT! sign, through the *Berliner Zimmer,* which had been fixed up as a family room. And then I stopped. And retraced my steps. I was standing in

136

front of Max's room again, the forbidden crypt. KEEP OUT! Hmm ... a little look wouldn't hurt, I thought. The last (and only) time I'd been in there, the day I met Maximilian, it was far too dark in the room to see anything.

I pressed down the handle and opened the door. It creaked.

Who knows what I expected? An altar in honor of the devil? A shrine for Frankenstein's monster? A cavernous room with walls painted in black?

What I found was a plain old kid's room stuffed with all-American boy paraphernalia, with sports and college pennants, collector's cars, an autographed baseball mitt, ice skates hanging from the door handle, a *Star Wars* calendar, a poster of the soon-to-be-released movie *Titanic*, the cruise liner plunging into a menacing sea. I stumbled over a book lying on the floor. I put my glass on a chest of drawers and picked the book up. It was the heavy, black, linen-bound volume I had seen Max reading the day I met him. *Sein und Schein* was the title in gold lettering, *Modern Stories for Students of German*. A German book? I flipped through it. It was in German. *German?* Max's name was written on the title page. Here and there passages were underlined with highlighter. Some of the words were even translated—and in Max's handwriting. Was it possible that he could read German? The book was dog-eared. Obviously *someone* had been reading it. Wouldn't that be just like Max to pull the wool over everyone's eyes...?

137

I stood up. It was getting late. If he didn't come home now, I'd go. I reached out for my glass on the chest. A dozen basketball trophies and a few framed photographs were positioned on the chest top. I picked up one of the pictures. It was a photograph of a much younger and smiling Max, holding a basketball, with a man. His coach? Or his father? The same man was in another picture with Max and Melissa. It was probably the father. But Max never spoke about him. Well, he never spoke about anything, for that matter...

"What the hell are you doing in here?"

I swung around, frightened by Max's sudden voice. I was so startled, the picture flew out of my hands, knocked over my drink, and landed in a puddle on the floor.

"Look what you did!" Maximilian said. "I told you to stay out!"

It did not look good. There was shattered glass all over the place, the photograph was turning brown from the soda, and the wooden frame was cracked.

"I'm sorry," I said. "I'm so sorry." I bent down and fished the photograph out of the puddle, but Max grabbed my arm and tore the picture out of my hand.

"Don't you dare touch that! Give it to me." He yanked me up and shoved me toward the door. "Get out!"

"I said I was sorry."

"Get out!" he said.

138

And I was out.

He slammed the door in my face. Just like in the movies, the KEEP OUT! sign swung back and forth in front of my nose.

"Well, I'm sick of you anyway," I screamed at the door. "I'm sick of your cynicism. And I'm sick of your morbidness! I'm sick of looking at your grotesque, repugnant, loathsome face! I quit!"

The door swung open.

"Aren't we using big words today?" he practically spit in my face. "Let me tell you something, kiddo. This is life, not a vocabulary test!"

Our faces were so close, I could smell a falafel he must have eaten shortly before.

"And for your information, Little Miss IQ," he said, "the word's morbidity, not morbidness."

For a nanosecond I wondered if he were right, but I zapped through my built-in dictionary and reassured myself that I wasn't mistaken. "For *your* information," I said, "you're wrong. You can use both. Either/or. Morbidity or morbidness. And you know what? I'm sick of both. I'm sick of your morbidity. And I'm sick of your morbidness! So there!"

Max was still leaning in so close, I felt compelled to take a step backward. But then he took a step forward. And then I took one backward. On and on, until he had me cornered against a wall. Now it was just me, Max, and the wall.

"What do I care if you quit?" he said. "You probably only agreed to tutor me because you thought I'd help you with basketball so you could go to England and spy on Prince William. Prince William! That's the most simplistic, asinine, preposterous, imbecilic thing I've ever heard!"

"Look who's using big words now."

"Do you know what your story is with him? You're scared of boys. You're scared of someone holding your hand, of someone touching you, of someone even just *looking* at you. So you moon over some stupid prince where the chances of you even meeting him are like a zillion to one. But that lets you off the hook. And you can stay pure and cerebral and no one can say you didn't try."

I can't remember exactly how I felt about what he said. But I do remember I wanted to get out of there. And fast. I grabbed my jacket and my backpack. "I don't have to listen to this."

"Where are you going? Home to Papa? He's not there."

"What are you talking about?"

"For being smart, you're pretty stupid."

"What's that supposed to mean?"

Max looked at me as if I truly had just landed on Earth from some alien planet. "He's out bonking my mother."

I have no idea where they came from, but suddenly they were there: tears. They were rolling down my cheeks, my neck, crawling into my collar and down my chest. "Bonking your mother?" I blubbered. "My father's bonking your mother?"

I had never used the word *bonk* before in my life. Although I wasn't altogether certain that I knew what it meant, it didn't sound like something I wanted my father to be doing with his mother.

I thrashed my way to the door.

"Grow up!" I heard Max say as I slammed the door behind me.

I don't remember how I got home—that's how upset I was. My memory doesn't kick in until about twenty meters from the gas station ruins. One of the street kids, the Poet, the one with the jeans jacket that had all the writing on it, stood up and looked my way. I didn't think anything of it. And neither was I suspicious when the Serpent, the guy with the peroxided hair and the snake tattoos, rose from his blanket.

"Hey, you, gotta mark?" asked the Serpent when I got closer.

"Come on, leave her alone," said the Poet. "She's just a kid."

"Ever see her mother? A megababe," said the Serpent, sauntering over to me. "You, too?"

"I'm sorry, but I don't have any money on me," I said.

The Serpent reached out in my direction. "What's in that backpack?"

"Hey, Marco, leave her alone," said the Poet, stepping between us, holding him back.

141

The situation was getting a little more complicated than I had originally thought. I was about to go when I realized that with his back to me, I could finally read the poem on the Poet's jacket. So I stopped. If I had left, my life would probably have continued along its due course. But I didn't leave, and my life was never the same again.

The Serpent took my hesitancy as an opportunity to push the Poet away and come at me again. I must say, I wasn't scared. Not for a second. Perhaps it was naive of me, but I wasn't. In fact, I actually even resented it when I heard a voice roar, "Don't touch her!" behind me. The voice spoke English. It was Maximilian. What the hell was *he* doing here?

I doubt the Serpent or the Poet could speak English, but the expression in Max's voice was unequivocal. The Poet cringed. The Serpent licked his lips. Two of the Mohawk Indians came over to see what all the commotion was about.

"Who and what the hell are *you*?" said the Serpent to Max in German, his chest expanding, ogling at white-faced, spiderwebbed, gooey-haired Max. The other boys surrounded Max from all sides. Clearly they did not like him.

"You looking to get your balls busted?" asked one of the Mohawks.

"Go, Nelly!" Max commanded.

What an idiot, I thought. Why the hell did he have to interfere like some Tarzan? But now that he had butted in, he left me no other alternative but to run.

So I ran. But after a few steps I decided to stay and take cover behind a car. I saw the Serpent shove Max. And then, within seconds, they made mincemeat out of him.

Max was leaning on me. He was heavy. The worst part was climbing the four flights to my apartment.

"This should never have happened," I said. "What did you want to prove? You almost got yourself killed."

"I almost got *myself* killed?" Max said. "How about you? Are you blind, or just stupid? You never heard of the word *mug*? *Rape*? *Attack*?"

"I know how to take care of myself," I said, admittedly a little less certain than a moment before.

Max was trying to catch his breath.

"Well, it's all your fault," I went on, making a weak attempt to defend myself.

"My fault? You're the one who ran away."

"You're the one who yelled at me!"

"You went in my room!"

"You were late!"

"You were too early!"

We stopped for a moment on the landing between floors, panting, and then went up to my apartment.

I fumbled for my keys. "Maybe I can get you into my room without bothering Risa. I think my mother's out."

Max nodded. God, he looked awful. His nose was swollen and the skin around his eyes was puffy, but because of the whiteface, I couldn't really see if it was already turning black and blue or green or purple or whatever color it's supposed to turn. And there was blood to see, of course, some of it still drippy-ish, most of it already caked.

Exhausted, Max leaned against the door. His elbow accidentally pressed against the bell. *Bbrriiiing!*

Within seconds we heard footsteps. The door swung open.

Risa looked at Max. Then at me. Then back to Max. *"Oy gevalt,"* she said.

Risa decided Max wouldn't need stitches, so why go to the hospital? She let me boil the water and get the towels, the gauze, Band-Aids, the medication, shampoo, and a bottle of cognac. And then she sent me out of the room. She'd perform the operation alone, she said. And let me tell you, I was *glad* she kicked me out. All the way in the kitchen I could hear Max's groans. It wasn't amusing. I made a mental note not to pursue a career in medicine or nursing.

Over an hour later, after Risa had doctored, bathed, and shampooed Max, she ushered me back into my room. It was dark inside. Risa said she had dimmed the lights because the glare hurt Max's eyes. But I think she turned down the lights so I wouldn't be able to see how awful he looked.

Max was sitting up in bed. I was afraid to look at his face, so I concentrated on his black leather pants

144

juxtaposed against my pink percale sheets with the tiny rosettes. Then I looked at his arms. They seemed okay. The sleeves of his black shirt were rolled up, and I could make out the tiny dark blond hairs on his arm. I didn't see any broken bones poking through his skin.

And then I looked at his face.

I was so startled, I actually gasped.

Risa laughed. "Who would have known?" she said. "There was a boy under all that makeup. Right, Nelly?"

The whiteface foundation was gone. The white, and the goo, and the black spiderweb designs, too. All that was left was a face. It was beat up, scratched, lacerated, and puffy, but it was a face all the same. Max's face. Two eyes, a nose, a mouth. Two ears. And hair. Blond hair. Thick, wavy, shampooed blond hair. And blue eyes. Very blue eyes.

"Boo," Max said.

I may have smiled.

"Hi," he said, softer. "Hi."

"You followed me home," were the first words I said to Max once Risa had left us alone in my room. "How come?"

He shrugged. "I don't know. I wanted to apologize. I guess I felt like a heel."

"Because of what you said about my father."

"Yeah. And because I got so angry."

"And because of what you said about me."

145

"No."

"No, what?"

"No, I did not feel bad about what I said about you. It was the truth."

I flushed. "You're a real sweetheart."

He tried to smile, but his lips were on strike.

"So if I understand correctly," I said, "you feel bad because what you said about my father *wasn't* the truth."

"You assume incorrectly. It was the truth. I just felt bad that I told you."

"How sensitive of you. How honest of you."

"Hey, I'm an honest guy."

"Really? So why are you pretending you don't know German?"

Max's eyes bulged for a second. It was only a second, but it was enough to know I'd hit the jackpot.

"The night we met, I saw you reading a book," I said. "The black book with the gold lettering. And when I was in your room, I saw it and it had your translation notes in it."

"You're a real snoop, you know?"

"I wasn't snooping! I was just bored. And then when I was in your room and stumbled over the book I was curious and I looked at it. And—"

I stopped midsentence, for something had just occurred to me. I hadn't planned on using my discovery as a means toward an end, but I realized suddenly what a gold mine it was. Maybe I *could* get Max to coach me yet. Hello, England!

"And?" Max said defiantly.

"And I thought that I might mention to your mother that you've been lying about your knowledge of German. And she might be so angry that she won't let you go to New York for the Christmas holidays. However, if you coach me in basketball, I might think twice about—"

"Is this blackmail?" he interrupted. "It won't work. She already knows I speak German."

"She knows? How?"

"Because she taught it to me when I was a kid. Didn't she tell you that?"

I vaguely remembered something of the sort. "So why did she ask me to tutor you?"

"She assumed I forgot most of it. You're not the only one who assumes incorrectly."

I frowned. "I see. So you don't need me anymore for German lessons?"

"I *never* needed you, kiddo. For anything."

"Well, then," I said, "if you don't need me anymore, I'll stop tutoring you in German."

"Fine with me."

"I stop tutoring you in German, *but* we don't tell your mother. She thinks I'm still tutoring you, pays me ten marks an hour, you teach me basketball instead, and *you* pocket the money."

"You never give up, do you?" He laughed. If I hadn't known he was in pain, I'd have thought he was enjoying himself.

I looked at him a moment or two, trying to figure

out my next move. It was strange seeing someone, a boy, stretched out on my bed like that. I was suddenly aware of how long his legs were and how the air in my room smelled different. Was it the leather from Max's pants? Or his socks? Or just him?

And whenever he opened his mouth, I sniffed out cognac. Had Risa given it to him against the pain?

Max shifted his weight, and I remembered I had a problem to solve. "Okay," I said. "If the money's not enough, I'll give you sex."

I wasn't completely convinced that I'd keep my side of the bargain, but at least I'd get a response out of him—or so I thought.

Max's eyes appeared to widen for a fraction of a second, but he said nothing.

"Did you hear?" I said. "You win. Sex."

He wasn't even looking at me. Was he deaf?

"Sex," I said. "I said, okay, I'll give you sex."

Max turned to me. "Okay. When's your mother due home?"

My heart stopped dead. "Now?" I said, my voice cracking. "You want it *now*?"

Max leaned in toward me. Closer and closer. Inch by inch. I ceased breathing.

Then, just a breath away from me, he stopped, twisted around, and got out of the bed. "I'll take the money instead," he said. "Tomorrow at four."

What? No sex?

I swallowed hard. Was I relieved or disappointed? I think I was both.

I watched Max grab his jacket and swing it over his shoulder. It fell against his back with a thud.

He left my room.

It was ten-thirty. The moon was out.

One-fifteen. I'd been sitting in my armchair in front of the window for hours. The moon had floated to the far corner of my window frame. My father still wasn't home.

I swear, I just didn't know *what* to think about my father and Melissa. Did my mother know? It struck me that she probably didn't, and that I should feel sorry for her. And I did. But I was also angry at her for allowing it to happen. If she hadn't been so crabby, if she hadn't let her thighs get all vein-marked and wobbly, maybe he wouldn't have deceived her. Some part of me knew I was being terribly unfair to her, but I couldn't help myself. Another part of me understood my father. Who couldn't help but fall in love with Melissa? But the thought of them together was nonetheless thoroughly disconcerting. And that made me angry. Angry at my father. And it made me sick to my stomach, too. Once, when the image of him and Melissa in the pantry overcame me, I ran to the toilet because I thought I was going to throw up. But I didn't, although I *did* have a bad case of hiccups for about a half hour after that.

My only comfort that night was that I was at least going to learn how to play basketball.

I was tired. I switched on my night-table lamp, got into my pajamas, and went to the closet to hang up my clothes. I was suddenly aware of William standing there, so majestic in his three-piece, dark blue, pinstriped, cashmere-blend suit. I went to him. The top of my head reached his collar bone. I got my footstool and stepped up. That was better.

"Hi," he said. "Hi."

And then he kissed me. It was perfect. It was tingly and warm and I could feel the tingles and the warmth rushing through me to my toes, my finger-tips, back up to my ears, down to my stomach, all over. William put his arms around me, and I rested my head on his chest, nestling into his embrace like a gently purring kitten rubbing its back against a velvety blanket. He lifted my chin. And he kissed me. Again.

And then there was a knock on the door.

I scrambled into bed, grabbing my basketball book. "Yes?" I said. "Come in."

It was my father. I stole a look at Prince William. Oh, no! His mouth was wet with saliva. I prayed my father wouldn't notice.

"I saw the light," my father said. "Just wanted to say good night." He sat down on my bed. "It's a little late to be reading, isn't it?"

Normally I would have hugged him. But I didn't feel like it. So I shrugged instead.

My father bent down and gave me a kiss.

And then I smelled him. Smoke. Liquor. Perfume.

Melissa's perfume. The stupidest mistake in the book.

"You smell funny," I said. "Like perfume."

"You mean my new cologne?"

I looked at him straight in the eyes. "I don't know. Maybe."

He evaded my stare and picked up my basketball book. "Find anyone to help you?" he said.

"Yes," I said. "Max. Max is going to help me."

The sudden joy in my voice surprised even me.

9

Educating Nelly

Max had ten days to get me in shape. It was clearly not enough time. Ten weeks, perhaps ten months, better yet ten *years,* would have been more like it. I was aware of the problem, of course, but I tried not to think about it. Max, however, kept on reminding me.

"For Christ's sake, you can't even dribble!" Max said the first day out on the court. The second day out on the court, he was still saying it. Intellectually I knew what I had to do: I had to bounce the ball with my fingertips, not the palm of my hand; I had to shoot layups by hitting the square on the backboard first; I had to keep the ball close to me; I had to watch the court, not the ball. I knew it. I did! I did! But invariably my whole hand would want to cup the ball, or I'd forget that the backboard existed. I'd keep the ball close to me when I was stationary, but the second I moved, the ball was gone. Or, if I did manage to dribble, I'd inadvertently look at the ball for a fraction of a second and then find myself colliding with Max, or banging into a fence, or tripping over a twig.

It was a good thing Max insisted on all the extras: knee protectors, ankle wraps, wristbands, sturdy sneakers, a mouthpiece. Without them I would have been a case for the emergency room. Or worse: for the mortuary. My father, pleased to see me getting along with Max and getting in shape at the same time, paid for all the paraphernalia. My mother, on the other hand, was a bit less supportive. Although I believe she actually enjoyed seeing me all sweaty in gym shorts and a tank top, my face flushed, hair slipping out of my braid, she was suspicious of my intentions. And whenever I mentioned Max, it was clear that our friendship made her uncomfortable. I could see it, the way her mouth would squish up and her nose twitch. In short, to my mother, basketball seemed to be adding insult to injury. Plus, it wasn't getting me any closer to my bat mitzvah, either.

Additional friction hit the fan when Melissa Minsky announced that her restaurant was to open on the evening of Saturday, October 25, the same day as my bat mitzvah. My mother was in a rage.

"That bitch," I heard her say to her girlfriend Becky Bernstein the TV talk show hostess, on the phone. "That stinker. That skunk."

My father tried to straighten things out, but failed. "She wanted to change the date when she realized the mistake," he told us, "but the news was already out. The invitations were printed. What could she do?"

"Print new invitations," said my mother.

My father sighed.

"Well, don't for a second think you're going to leave in the middle of Nelly's bat mitzvah party to go play at Minsky's!" she hissed.

"What do you take me for?" my father said, storming out of the house. "She's my daughter!"

And me? The daughter? I tried to ignore them. As best I could, at any rate. And besides, I knew they'd calm down soon enough. They always did. More or less.

On the third day out on the court, after a particularly trying session, Max made a decision that changed the course of my life.

"Hey, you, get over here," Max said with his phony Italian Brooklyn accent. He'd gotten into the practice of talking to me like a Mafia heavyweight, something he'd picked up from watching too many De Niro movies, I think. But I got a kick out of it, and he knew it, too.

"Are you deaf or what? I said get over here!" Max De Niroed.

I walked across the basketball court, overheated, out of breath, my feet sweaty, my toes numb, confined as they were in my sneakers. I was lightheaded, but aware that it was chilly outside. Cold air nipped faintly at the tip of my nose and settled on the top of my cheeks. It was almost dark outside and the toddlers in the playground behind the basketball court were getting cranky. The moms were strapping them into strollers and stuffing zwieback into their mouths to shut them up.

"Move that butt," Max said.

I was about two meters from him when he suddenly flung the ball at me. It bashed into my stomach. I doubled up and it rolled away.

"That hurt!" I said.

"I thought you were going to catch it, for Christ's sake. I'm sorry."

I picked up the ball.

Max exhaled heavily. I could tell he was trying to choose his words carefully. I looked at his face. It was still a little swollen, and the skin around his eyes had turned a myriad of colors ranging from yellow, to blue, to purple. There was a Band-Aid on his right cheekbone. His lips were still a little puffy. And although the ring in his nose and the whiteface were gone, his hair was back to sticking straight up as if it had been electrocuted. And he still wore black. Despite the getup, I could tell that the kids in school thought he looked cool. It didn't matter to me one way or the other. All I knew was that I needed a basketball coach because I needed to get on the girls' basketball team, because I needed to get to the basketball playoffs in England, because I needed to get to William.

It was that simple.

"I don't think we're getting anywhere," Max said.

I knew that was coming.

"I can't help you," he went on. He was talking in his normal Max Minsky voice, so I knew he meant business. "This was your last lesson. I'll return your money."

My heart was in my throat, hammering away so fast, I was sure I'd choke on it.

"Maybe there's another way of getting you to England," he said. "A junior astronomers' conference or something."

"But I want to go with the basketball team."

"Why, for Christ's sake?"

"Because!"

He got up. "It's getting cold. Let's get out of here."

He started walking toward the exit. "Can't you just take a shopping trip to London? Go for the weekend. With your mother. Go to Harrods and Oxford Street, have tea and biscuits somewhere, and then drop by Buckingham Palace. He might be home."

"Don't make fun of me. That's not what this is about!" My voice was at least two octaves higher than usual. "Do you understand? That's not what it's about!"

He swung around. "Then what *is* it about? Are you a glutton for punishment? A masochist? A dimwit? Because you're certainly not a basketball player!"

"I can do it. I *know* I can do it." I was banging my thighs with my fists.

"You can't, Nelly! Not in a week! You've got no talent for this. Face up to it."

"I can, goddamn it! I can!" I started to cry.

I was angry at myself. I didn't want to cry. I wanted to be strong. Tough. "I can!" I said. "And I will. I'm going to prove it. I'm going to prove it to you, to everyone at school. To my mother. I can do it! Do you hear?"

Max heaved the basketball at me. It almost knocked me over.

"You bastard!" I said, and threw the ball back in his face.

"Not at me, you idiot!" He threw the ball back to me. "At the stupid basket. Throw it at the stupid basket!"

I threw it at the stupid basket.

It hit the rim, popped up, and—

"Rebound!"

I lunged forward and jumped up, but missed the ball. It crashed down next to me and bounced up. I managed to catch it on its way down.

"Get rid of it!" Max said. "Shoot!"

I aimed, thrust the ball, and watched it fly through the hoop. I reached out to catch it before Max could

157

yell at me again, but Max was faster. He appeared out of nowhere, sprang up, caught the ball, dribbled to the basket, and—*whop!*—I bopped the ball out of his hands. Max turned to me, surprised. I dribbled the ball away from him, one bounce, two bounces, but then it was gone. Max had it. And then it was flying through the air. And then it was slipping through the basket. It bounced down and rolled away. Max went after it. I let him. I stood watching, breathing heavily. And then Max was back.

"I want you to know, you little nerd, that any dumb five-year-old with a minimum amount of co-ordination can do what you just did," he said. "And better." He chucked the ball at me.

I caught it.

"Same place, same time tomorrow," he said. "I just hope Prince William knows to appreciate what I'm doing for him."

Max turned away and ran to the gate.

I caught up to him a minute or two later.

"Thanks," I said.

He barely looked at me. "Don't pride yourself on anything. I thrive on challenges."

We walked in silence a moment or two. Then Max, grinning, said, "You know, you're one angry kid."

"What? Did you think you had a monopoly on anger?"

Max slapped the basketball out of my hands and started bouncing it. He ran down the street doing a fancy dribble, making figure eights between his legs with the ball. It looked very professional, very hard to master, absolutely intimidating.

"Showoff!" I said.

"It's a skill. I needed it. I was a point guard," he said. "Like Nick van Exel."

"Like Nick who?"

Max sighed. I knew what he was thinking: How could I play basketball if I didn't know anything about it?

He did a couple more figure eights, dribbling around me, teasing me.

"Stop!" I shouted, laughing, but understanding for the first time the enormity of our task ahead.

"Dribbling between your legs is good against anger," he said, stopping. "You should try it some time."

"Ha. Ha."

"My mother says my getup was my way of demonstrating my pent-up aggression. She says I'm angry at her for divorcing my father and bringing me to Berlin."

"Are you?"

"You bet!"

I smiled and Max looked away. "Well, at least the Berlin part," he said. "My father's another story."

We were at the corner. The light turned red. I buttoned up my jacket. The summer was over. I could feel it. Max nervously bounced the ball, waiting for the light to change. "I miss my dad," he suddenly said. "Don't ask me why. I can see, you know, why she came here. She had to get away from him. And from New York. But then I think: why'd she have to schlep *me* along?"

The light turned green.

"It wasn't scary dressing up like that?" I asked.

"It was itchy. I think I'm allergic to that makeup. My skin broke out. I'm allergic to a lot of things."

"I mean, weren't you asking for a lot of trouble?"

"You seem so interested. Are you thinking of pursuing a career in psychiatry?"

I clasped my hands to my heart. "I'm only trying to help you," I said theatrically.

"I did it mostly at home," he said. "For my mom." He gave me a friendly punch on my shoulder. "And for you. And that one day at school. It was like in acting class. I was playing a part. I like doing that. Dressing up for different parts. I'm going to be an actor when I grow up—if I ever grow up. I was in the drama club at school, did you know?"

"Really?"

"You should have seen me in *Our Town*. I was a great George. All the girls cried when I buried my wife, Emily."

When I got upstairs, my father was in the dining room eating a chopped liver sandwich and Risa was walking in and out of the kitchen and the dining room, emptying the dishwasher and putting away the china.

160

I sat down and made myself a sandwich, too, spreading the liver in silence, listening to my father chomping away and then gulping it down. I was suddenly aware of all the noise he was making. I could practically hear the saliva in his mouth swishing the liver around. It sounded so crude. Did he make sounds like that with Melissa? For a second I tried to picture him with Melissa, but my brain refused to focus.

"Brrr," I said out loud, shivering at the thought of them.

My father looked up at me. "Did you say something?"

I shook my head, wondering if he knew that I knew his secret. And I wondered if my mother knew.

"So what have you been up to?" my father asked me.

I shook the thoughts of my father's love life out of my head. "I'm dirty and sweaty, wearing dirty and sweaty gym clothes, and you're asking me what I've been up to?"

"Excuse me, Your Grimy Highness."

I tried to smile. "We had a breakthrough today."

"Good for you. I'm proud of you, princess." He paused a moment. "I'm proud of you whether you get on that basketball team or not."

"Whether? I *will*."

My father reached over and kissed me on my forehead. He licked his lips. "Mmm. What's this I taste? Basketball slime?" He pretended to vomit. His mouth

161

opened wide and his tongue stuck out. "Blah."

I laughed, punching him in his arm. "You're disgusting!"

"Bubeleh, I want you to take a shower," said Risa, suddenly making her presence felt. "Such dirt. And look at those hands!"

I made a face, and she went back to the kitchen.

My father seemed suddenly earnest. "Princess, just because you want something doesn't mean you're going to get it. You know that, don't you?"

"Oh, Papa. I wasn't born yesterday. But even so, that doesn't mean that I should stop trying."

"Absolutely not."

"And if I try hard enough, I'll get what I want."

My father shook his head. "No, that's not the way it works. Where did you learn that? From your mother? From some silly American sitcom?"

My father grabbed his mug and took a slug of beer. He seemed upset. Had I hurt his feelings? Did he think I thought he didn't try hard enough and that's why he wasn't a successful musician?

Perhaps my father knew what I was thinking, because then he said, "Trying to get what you want, and knowing that you tried, *that's* what makes us happy. It's not the goal that's important, but the road we take to get where we want to go, and what we learn about ourselves on the way there."

"What crap," my mother said, entering the dining room and sitting down at the table. She looked at my father. "You sound like Kahlil Gibran. Beate may

162

be a pushover for it, but some people might think Nelly should be learning about how to get ahead in the world instead of listening to all that hippie schmaltz. If the goal's not important, why go out on the road in the first place? It's a waste of time."

How could she be so rotten? She just walks in and spoils the whole mood. And she doesn't even really believe in what she was saying, either. She likes a nice goal every now and then, sure, but she's all for learning along the way, too. I know it. What was eating her?

"I can't tell you what to do, princess," my father said to me, rising, ignoring my mother, "but whatever it is, enjoy." He took a gulp of his beer, picked up his mug and his dish, and without giving my mother as much as a look, he left the table. I noticed that his shirttails were flopping out of his pants.

When he was gone, my mother fell back in her seat. "Oh, God," she said. "Oh, God."

I think she started to cry, but I got up to wash my hands before I could tell for sure.

When I got back to the dining room, Risa and my mother were talking softly to each other. I listened a moment before entering.

"I don't know," my mother said. "I just don't know." Her voice sounded so tired. And bitter. "She was out again with that Minsky boy. When was the last time she practiced her Torah portion?"

"Lucy," Risa began, "I know you're worried about

a lot of things, not just Nelly—"

"So she hasn't worked on it this week?" my mother said, her voice louder, harsher.

I breezed in through the door and sat down. "I'm back."

"Nelly," my mother said to me. "Your bat mitzvah is just a few weeks away. You've got to think of priorities."

"Priorities?"

She wasn't in the mood for a conversation. She had a speech prepared. "You seem to have time for everything," she said. "For astronomy. For Pia. For books. School. For that prince of yours. And now for basketball." Her voice was threatening to crack. "And what about your bat mitzvah?"

Risa put her hand on my mother's shoulder. "Lucy, dear."

"Why spend so much time with basketball?" my mother said. "It doesn't seem to be getting anywhere."

"How do you know?" I shouted. "And what do you mean it's not getting anywhere? Where exactly is something supposed to 'get to' for you to approve of it?"

"Quiet! Both of you!" Risa said.

The authority in Risa's voice shut us up. Risa looked at me. "Nelly, beginning tomorrow, we are working a half hour every day on the Torah. No excuses. And no exceptions. And if you want to memorize the Magna Carta, you'll do it *after* you get the

Torah down pat."

I gulped. Risa never talked to me like that.

She turned to my mother. "And you, Lucy, I want you to please try to look at basketball as a kind of metaphor."

"Oh, Risa, please," said my mother, rising.

"Sit down!"

My mother sat down. It was good to know that there was someone around who could stand up to her.

"I read something I think you should know," Risa went on. "Are you listening?"

My mother rolled her eyes.

"Did you know that in the Midrash," Risa went on stubbornly, "they compare the Torah to a young girl's ball? A *ball*. They say, 'as a ball is tossed by hand from one child to another, so Moses received the Torah at Sinai and then passed it to Joshua, Joshua to the elders, the elders to the prophets. And then the prophets delivered it to the Great Synagogue.'"

My mother and I were perfectly still. When Risa talked, you listened. So we sat there, mesmerized by her words, her eyes, and her twinkling glass stone.

"Metaphorically speaking, a bat mitzvah means that it's time for the ball to be thrown to the young girl," Risa said softly, almost to herself. "So she has to know how to catch the ball and run with it, and then she has to know enough about how the ball is made, how it feels, how it spins and bounces, in order to be able to throw it to her children and the next generation of ball catchers." Risa looked up at my mother. "Do you understand, Lucy? Let Nelly play basketball. It'll make her a damn good catcher and a better thrower. We owe it to ourselves."

My mother and I sat there for a moment, dumb-founded. Neither of us, no one—probably not even God himself—had ever seen basketball as a Jewish metaphor. It was brilliant. Absolutely brilliant.

"Ha!" I said to my mother. "You see?"

"I had an idea last night," Max began the second he hit the court for practice. "Remember the between-the-legs dribble I did yesterday?"

"The figure eights?"

"I'm going to teach you how to do that," he went on.

I looked at him blankly.

"A couple of years ago," he said, "at basketball camp, my coach told us something I never forgot. He said that if you want to be chosen in a pick-up game, it pays to learn how to walk onto the court while dribbling between your legs."

I was beginning to understand.

"You get it?" he asked.

"I think so. You mean, if I dribble between my legs when I'm called onto the court, they'll think I'm really good?"

"Exactly."

"But if I'm not really good the rest of the game?"

"That could be a problem," he said, "so we'll

practice how to play, too. A little, at least. But if you wow them in one area the second you start and avoid making too much of a fool of yourself the rest of the time, you might possibly trick them into thinking you're good."

"But—"

"And besides, you can use this move during the game to protect the ball against a defender. The idea is to put yourself into a position during the game so you can use the move, kind of make sure your defender is on top of you. That's when it works best because—"

"But—"

"Because with this move your body acts as a natural shield and—"

"But—"

"But *what,* for Christ's sake?"

"But what if I can't do it? What if I can't dribble between my legs? It looks awfully intricate. Have you thought about that?"

"Of course I've thought of that. But it's your only chance, Nelly. Decide."

"Okay, you take the ball in your right hand."

I took the ball in my right hand.

"Now spread your legs a little wider," Max instructed.

I spread my legs a little wider.

"And now put your left leg forward," Max said, performing the move in slow motion.

I raised my left foot—almost losing my balance.

"Now, just before the left foot touches the floor, dribble the ball, guide it, from in front of your right foot into the space between your legs."

I started to guide the ball—and lost my balance.

"Don't do it yet! Just watch!"

I dropped the ball.

"And then intercept the ball with your left hand," he went on, "which is behind you, palm to your back, and bring the ball around your left foot and through your legs again."

He stood up straight. "Got it?"

Of course I *got* it. The problem was could I *do* it?

And I couldn't. Not that day. And not the day after. I watched Nick van Exel on tapes and still couldn't do it. I don't know how many times we drilled it. I stopped counting.

"Slow down," he hollered. "You're being sloppy. Once you get the natural flow, it'll speed up by itself."

I slowed down.

"Bend your knees!" he hollered.

"But why?" I cried out, exasperated.

"You'll be quicker if your knees are bent. And it'll be easier to change direction."

I bent my knees. And started from the top. And actually made two reasonably tidy figure eights.

"Again!" Max hollered.

I made three.

And then four.

"Okay," Max said. "So now the real work begins."

I had a couple of days left to perfect my act.

When I think about that next week today, I see it all in fast motion, like an ancient Charlie Chaplin movie where all the actors scramble around like chickens without heads. I wake up, go to school, dash home, dress for basketball, meet Max, practice, eat at least two portions of Melissa's *kasha varnishkes,* then Risa's cheesecake, get showered, race over to the residence home, practice my haftarah, analyze my Torah portion, play cards with Rosi Goldfarb, Helena Lewi, and Risa, feast on junk food. My mother zips in and out of my life saying good morning, how are you, good night. She has begun to drink schnapps before she goes to bed. She's looking for a TV job, for a magazine job, for my father. He's away most of the time, moving in and out of my life, too, playing his clarinet, working with his band, spending time with Melissa, I presume. I thrive nonetheless. I'm on a roll. Yvonne needles me and Anton glares at me, but who cares? I promise to write one last mystery lady letter to Anton for Pia. Max and I try our best to be patient with each other. I try to learn how to pass, defend, shoot. I'm improving. A little. I am. I really am. Max knows it. I know it. The basket knows it. The ball, too. Every once in a while it does what I want it to.

Max and Risa have become friends.

*   *   *

169

"Stop squirming," I heard Risa say as I entered the room. "And take off the sweatshirt."

Max was wearing baggy Bermudas and a floppy bright blue hooded sweatshirt with the high school insignia STUYVESANT. Under the sweatshirt he had on a tank top. His sleeveless arms swung self-consciously at his sides, endlessly long and slender.

Max must've felt my eyes on him, because he turned to me, but I looked away, embarrassed. I sat down and watched Risa take his measurements.

It was the afternoon before the big tryout basketball game. Risa had offered to sew Max a suit for his mother's opening. Apparently it was almost finished, but Risa had misplaced the index card with his measurements and wanted them for the record. While they fitted the suit, I was in my room secretly composing Pia's last letter to Anton. As far as I was concerned, it was a waste of time. In record-breaking speed, I wrote the letter, printed it out, stuck it in an envelope, addressed it, and threw it into my backpack to give to Pia the next day. I was eager to go downstairs for my last basketball lesson. But it didn't look like Risa and Max were in a hurry.

"Hmm," Risa said to Max. "You have the same measurements as my husband, Leopold, may he rest in peace." She winked at Max. "Nice build."

Max blushed, but I could tell he liked Risa's attention. And I could tell she liked teasing him. She stepped back and took another appraising look as Max slipped his sweatshirt back over his head.

"Do you miss him?" Max asked.

I've never seen Risa so startled. I don't think anyone in my family ever asked her that question, simple though it was. And I knew why no one asked: she didn't want us to.

Risa busied herself with her tape measure, and then said, "He died a long time ago. Over seven years ago."

"Oh?" said Max, obviously unsatisfied with her answer.

Risa met his eyes. "Of course I miss him. What do you think?"

I gave Max a signal to cool it. He understood.

"That's some beautiful gem," he said, changing the subject, pointing to Risa's glass stone.

I rolled my eyes. Max the lapidary. He probably didn't know the difference between a moonstone and a gallstone.

"Is it real?" he asked.

"Of course it's real. It's here, isn't it?" Risa said, teasingly, holding her stone out to him.

Max reached out and touched it. "I meant, is it real real. A diamond or something?"

"A diamond, he asks! *Kindchen,* I'd have retired to the French Riviera by now if this were a diamond. It's just glass, a family heirloom, passed down from generation to generation on the female side." She paused a moment, but then went on. "And since I have no children of my own, when the time comes I'm giving the stone to Nelly's mother, Lucy. Lucy's mother,

Hanna, Nelly's grandmother, was my childhood friend."

"It's cool," Max said a little self-consciously.

"Yes, it's beautiful. I've always thought so," I said, reminding them that I was in the room, too.

"When I was a child, my mother let me play with it," Risa said, smiling. "It reflected the light, and I liked to shine it into dark places where light barely came. It was a challenge to see if I could brighten something that was dark."

Risa wasn't looking at us. She was off somewhere else—in her head, where her memories were engraved in stone like the Ten Commandments.

"But then the war came," she said, "and there was no time for children's games. We went into hiding. And the stone went with us. It was our good-luck charm."

This was the first time I'd ever heard this story. I was amazed that Risa was even talking about it. The war. Hiding. Her parents. I turned to Max. He was sitting on the arm of Risa's Biedermeier couch.

"But then our luck ran out," Risa said, looking at me. "I wasn't much older than you when my parents and I were separated. It was a very dark time. But despite all the darkness around me, my loneliness and my fear of hunger and death, one day it occurred to me that I was at least *alive*. And that thought was like a sudden patch of light coming through the clouds. And it gave me hope. And this hope filled me and brightened the life of the people around me. And that's when it occurred to me that I could be just like the stone. I could reflect light, too."

Risa looked up at us. First at Max. And then at me. "And that's why I wear this all the time," she said. "As a reminder." She held my gaze for a couple of seconds. I wasn't sure if she was finished or not, if she wanted me to say anything or not. But there didn't seem to be anything for me to say, so I kept still. Max, too.

"Light is everywhere, Nelly," Risa said. "Even in darkness. We just have to find it and let it become a part of ourselves. And if we set our heart to it, we can learn to reflect it so others may find their way, too."

Exhausted, or so it seemed, Risa turned around and sat down on her sofa. "Now, I know that may all sound a little maudlin to you kids. But what can I say? I'm a sentimental old lady." She sat up straight. "So now you," she said to Max. "Do you miss your father?"

Startled, Max took a beat or two to gather his thoughts. Then he sat down next to her. "Yeah. Even though I never really spent much time with him. But I also miss my friends. And the World Series. And my shrink, Randolph. I spent plenty of time with *him*." Max laughed.

I bounced the ball a couple of times to let Risa and Max know I was ready to go. But Max didn't seem to care. "Why'd you move to Germany after the war?" he asked Risa. "I mean, how *could* you? After what the Germans did?"

Inwardly I cursed Max. No one ever talks to Risa about this.

"Leopold considered himself a German."

"So?"

"You ask hard questions, *Kindchen*. But I'll make it quick, so Little Miss Impatient can get out of here," she said, shooting me a look.

I stopped bouncing the ball.

Risa handed Max a silver tray with fine chocolates. "*Ess a bissel.*"

Max shook his head. "I'm allergic to chocolate."

Risa nodded. "Oh, a pity." She looked at me. "Here, take one."

I got up and took two. "Max's," I said.

Risa made a face and turned her attention back to Max. "Easy to explain it's not, especially not to someone like you who doesn't even want to be here. Leopold was offered a job in Berlin, a good one, and after the war, this was nothing to sneeze at. You must understand, we had nothing. Absolutely nothing. A pair of shoes. A shirt. A few pennies. But Leopold, he also had Berlin. This was his life, his city. The air he breathed. His culture. It's your mother's city, too. The way New York is yours. So Leo came back. And she came back. And maybe you'll go back to New York."

"But—"

"But what?—Augh. I know. I know. You want to know *how*? You want to know *how* could I? Well, why not, *Kindchen*? Why shouldn't we live here? Who the hell are they? Why shouldn't they see that they didn't kill all of us off?"

"Do you ever feel like a freak here?" Max asked me on the stairs going down. "Because you're Jewish? Like you're different from everybody else? Whenever I see old guys on the street, anyone who was old enough to carry a gun during the war, I think, 'Does he know I'm Jewish? Would he have killed me?' You don't think of stuff like that?"

I knew he'd ask me that eventually. They all do. All the new Jews in town.

"You remind me of my grandma Hanna," I said, opening the door to the street. "My mother's mother. She's dead now. But I remember once when she came to Berlin to visit us. I was maybe six. And we were out for a walk in the Tiergarten, just my grandmother and me, and then suddenly she stopped and pointed to this thin old man in a trench coat. He was smoking a cigarette and drinking a beer at a snack stand. And she said, 'Oh, my God, Nelly! It's Mengele. Dr. Mengele.'"

Max laughed. And I did, too. It was exhilarating, making someone laugh.

"Anyway," I went on, "I had no idea who Dr. Mengele was. At the time the only doctors I knew were my eye doctor, my dentist, and my pediatrician, and none of them were called Mengele. Anyway, when we got home, the first thing I told my mother was that we had seen Dr. Mengele smoking a cigarette in the Tiergarten. My mother was furious. She was so

175

angry at my grandmother. And then she sat me down, got my father, and said, 'Benny, this is *your* department. Tell her.' And then my father went into this whole spiel about how fifty years ago the Germans, people like Mengele, had done terrible things to people like Risa and Leopold in the concentration camps, and that they got away with it, that they escaped prosecution. And I asked him which Germans? And he said, 'The Nazis.' The word was vaguely familiar to me. I asked him what Nazis were exactly and he said, 'Bad Germans,' and I asked, 'Like Herr Pomplun, our landlord?' And he said he didn't know. Probably not. Then I asked him if my *oma* Anneliese and my *opa* Hans-Otto were Nazis. And he said, 'Don't be ridiculous!' which compelled my mother to say, 'But people they grew up with probably were.' "

Max and I walked on a few moments in silence. Then I stopped. "Why am I telling you this?"

"I asked you if you felt like a freak."

"Oh, right. No, I don't. At least not because of being Jewish. There are enough of us around. Not a lot, but enough."

"You're not like scared? There's stuff in the paper all the time. You're not worried that someone's going to blow up your bat mitzvah reception or something?"

"Oh, God! My mother would have a heart attack. All the floral arrangements up in smoke!"

Max laughed so loud I felt like I was the new Jerry Seinfeld.

"But no," I said, "I always forget to be scared. You know, there's a bunch of Jews in school. It's pretty normal there. We even have a Judaism class. Have you met Anton Weissenberger yet? His father's a rabbi."

"You mean Schwarzenegger?" Max flexed his right arm.

"Exactly."

We both smiled. As if we were conspirators. As if we had been friends for years and years and knew exactly what the other was thinking—like me and Fiona used to be and the way we agreed we'd never accept little brains, big breasts, or an MCM handbag.

"And there are a lot of American Jews in school, too," I said. "Like Yvonne. Yvonne Cohen. You've met *her*."

I thought Max would smile conspiratorially with me again, but he didn't. In fact, he evaded my eyes and I felt my stomach knot up. But it was just for a split second, and when he looked back at me, my stomach relaxed.

"But I'll tell you something," I said. "I'm glad that I'm half American—but don't you dare tell my mother!"

Max cupped his hand to his ear as if he were making a phone call. "Hello, Frau Edelmeister, this is the secret police. We have reason to believe that your daughter—"

"Wait a second! Let me specify." I laughed. "I

mean, it's not so much that I'm thrilled that I'm American. I could be anything. Anything, as long as I'm not one hundred percent German."

Max looked at me skeptically, then cupped his ear again. "Hello, Frau Edelmeister? Are you listening to this? I think this is important." He held his hand up to my mouth like a microphone.

I tried to choose my words carefully. "Germans aren't allowed to like themselves. The German kids today, they got an awful deal. They live with a permanent bad conscience that—"

"Oh, such terrible pangs of guilt!"

"Shhh! Listen! Imagine if you were always being reminded that in the not so distant past you and your friends were the bad guys. The really bad guys. German kids are always being reminded about how terrible their grandparents were, what butchers they were, or weaklings, or opportunists. I mean, I think they *should* be reminded. It's only two generations ago. And it's their grandparents, for God's sake. And they *were* butchers. But then on the other hand, I'm glad *I* don't have to deal with the guilty conscience. At least not one hundred percent. It's a load."

"Oh, poor German kids," Max said. "Boo hoo. Boo hoo."

"It's not like it's their fault, Max. They inherited it. Like a weak bladder."

"You've given this a lot of thought."

"I live here. I can't help it. It comes with the territory. But don't get me wrong. I don't mind living here. I like it. I *love* it. I mean, it's my home. Right?"

"You think a lot. Don't you?"

I blushed. "I'm a freak. Arrest me."

"It was a compliment."

My cheeks were going to dissolve from the heat they were producing. I bounced my ball a couple of times. "I used to feel like more of a freak, but the past two weeks have been different."

"That's because you're taking in the fresh air," he said like a schoolmarm, suddenly grabbing the basketball out of my hand and running across the street, hooting.

I ran after him.

We ran all the way to the playground, hit the basketball court, and kept on running, falling into a game of Around the World and then 5-3-1 for a warm-up. I moved around the court in a semicircle shooting baskets, missing most, right layup, right corner, right wing, top of the key, on and on in orbit around the basket and then back, shooting, catching, aiming, rebounding. I was far better at figure eights, but I made a couple of baskets. Who knows? Maybe I *would* be able to fool the people at the game into thinking I could play.

Like two ice skaters performing compulsory figures, we shifted intuitively into a drill mode, first the offense drills—passing, dribbling, jump-shots—then the defense exercises. Max dribbled down court and I tried to stop him. I couldn't. Then I dribbled downcourt making figure eights, the ball between my legs. He stopped me, but only after my fifth figure eight. Then we scrimmaged. My arms, fingers, and legs did all the work. My brain was out to lunch. I shuffled and dribbled and jumped, danced around the court, lost the ball, got it back, fouled, made a steal. We didn't rest once. I couldn't have, even if I'd wanted to. I was going too fast to stop, flying, whizzing, breezing as I was through the court. It remains a mystery, but something happened out there on the court that day. Something loosened deep inside me, something that had been holding me back all those years. And suddenly — or so it seemed — I was a different Nelly, a Nelly who actually knew how to *move*.

But then: *whuunk!* Something stopped me mid-jump. Banged into me. A wall. A force. A body. It was Max. His hands were gripping my shoulders, holding me steady. His sweatshirt was off. He was breathing hard.

I was breathing hard, too. And loud. My glasses were sprinkled with wet. My cheeks were aflame. My braid had apparently unloosened, because I felt strands of hair tickling my face.

"It's raining," Max said.

I tried to catch my breath.

We were standing close, so close I felt the heat of Max's body. Beads of perspiration, like a string of tiny diamonds, lined his upper lip. Dazed, I watched him gently raise his hand. Was he going to touch me?

My heart was pounding so wildly, I was certain it was going to collapse from exhaustion. Was it pounding from physical exertion or from the anticipation of Max's touch?

Finally, miraculously, I felt the very tips of Max's fingertips graze my forehead. And then with agonizing slowness he softly brushed the stray hair from my face.

"You're okay," Max said. "You'll be fine. Just fine."

Later, before dinner, I fell asleep looking out at the evening sky. When I opened my eyes again, I rose from my armchair and floated skyward into the velvety darkness of the night. I knew Prince William would be there. And there he was, poised among millions of twinkling orbs of light. But something was different. He'd changed his clothes. His dark blue, pinstriped, cashmere-blend suit was gone. He now wore baggy Bermuda shorts and a floppy, bright blue hooded sweatshirt. But we kissed anyway. As always.

10
The BLaCK HOLe

They say nothing escapes a black hole, not even light. Once you get sucked in, you're gone, everything's gone, time, space, you. *Adieu.*

But then again, some cosmologists point out that Einstein's theories suggest that if you fell into a black hole, you wouldn't be killed but might pass through wormholes, tunnels that link one part of space-time with another to reach some other universe, another part of our universe, or another time.

Metaphorically speaking, I like to think that that's what happened to me: I got sucked into a black hole, was then vacuumed through a wormhole, and got blasted out at the other end, where I was catapulted into another part of the universe, my universe, our universe, yes, but new and strange all the same.

The black hole had been sucking me in for weeks. I just didn't know it. I didn't know it until I sat down to dinner that evening.

"Max says I'll be fine at the tryouts tomorrow," I announced to my mother and father. Just thinking about my last basketball lesson made me feel all warm and woozy inside. "The game starts at four. The big gym."

"Sorry, honey," my mother said. "Herr Lerner set up a meeting with a producer for tomorrow. I couldn't get out of it."

I was actually disappointed. I suppose I wanted my mother to witness my glory more than I had imagined. Without her, my victory would only be half as sweet. And anyway: Did she *really* have an appointment, or was that just an excuse?

"But Risa promised she'd be there," said my mother. "And your father—"

"Are you worried that I'll embarrass you?" I said, cutting her off.

"Embarrass me? Nelly, what are you talking about? You never embarrass me."

"May I quote you on that for future reference?"

"You aggravate me. You drive me crazy. You make me want to scream. But you don't embarrass me."

"But you don't want to come, either."

"I *want* to come, but I can't. There's a difference. I promise to be at your first game." She winked at me and crossed her fingers. "Okay?"

I looked at my father.

"I didn't know it was tomorrow…" he said, his voice trailing off. He evaded my eyes.

My mother banged her fork down. "My excuse is legitimate. What's yours?" Her voice was unusually high-pitched.

My father just stared ahead.

My mother sprang up with her plate. For a second I thought she was going to smash it in his face the way they throw seven-layer whipped-cream cakes in people's faces in the movies. But she didn't. "The bat mitzvah caterer will be here soon," she said, fairly under control, going to the dishwasher.

"Does he make *kasha varnishkes*?" I asked, meaning to add a little levity into the conversation.

"*Kasha varnishkes*? I don't think so. No," she said. "Since when do you want *kasha varnishkes*?"

"I had some at Melissa's and I thought—"

My mother whipped around. "At Melissa's?"

My father put his hand on his forehead and dropped his head.

"Why not?" I said. "She's a cook."

My mother practically threw her plate into the dishwasher.

"It's only a suggestion, Mom. I thought maybe we could have *kasha varnishkes* at the buffet."

"No!"

"No? Why not?"

"Because I said so!"

I jumped up. "Because *you* said so? Why is nothing

184

I ever do or ever say right? It always has to be the way *you* want it." I was fighting tears. I kicked the chair instead. "Well, whose bat mitzvah is this, anyway? You tell me to take an interest in the preparations and when I do, you yell at me. I'm sick of it!"

"Oh, Nelly!" my mother said.

My tears made it hard for me to see, but I made it to the door okay. And I was out.

"Oh, God!" I heard my mother say. "Oh, God. I'm so unfair to her."

She was coming after me. I heard my father's chair make a scratchy sound on the kitchen tiles. He was coming, too. I ran into my room, slammed the door, and fell on my bed. They were in the hall.

My father must've reached out to touch my mother, perhaps put his hand on her shoulder, because suddenly I heard her snap at him, "Don't touch me, you bastard!"

"Lucy," he said.

"Lucy, what? What?"

I put a pillow over my head, squashed it over my ears. But I could still hear.

"What do you want to say?" my mother screamed. "Just come out and say it."

"Lucy, I..."

"Lucy, I what? Do you want me to finish the sentence for you, too? Lucy, I don't love you anymore? Lucy, I am in love with someone else? Lucy, I am so sorry I humiliated you? Lucy, I *what,* goddamn it, what!"

185

I stopped crying. My mother was doing enough of a job for the two of us.

"Things don't always turn out the way we want them to," my father said. "They just don't."

"You're damn right they don't! I bet you thought you were going to have a pleasant evening at home. Well, you're not. Because I'm kicking you out of the house. Right now. So go look for a bed at your girlfriend Melissa's. And if she won't have you, I'm sure Beate will!"

I stopped breathing.

Beate! What did Beate have to do with this? My mother's ex-best friend, Beate, the actress?

"Beate?" my father said.

"Yes, Beate!" said my mother. "What, in God's name, do you take me for?"

"Lucy," my father said, lowering his voice, "Nelly can hear us."

"I don't give a damn if she can hear us. Let her know. She probably does already."

I didn't. I didn't know. Beate?

"Let her know what a jerk you are," she said. "And what a jerk I am."

And then she started to really cry. It was more than crying—it was gulping and gasping. Blubbering. In any case, it sounded pretty sloppy.

And then I heard something that made my hair stand up. It was my father. And he was crying, too. I'd never heard him cry. It was like a moan. "Lucy, Lucy, I'm sorry," he said over and over again.

My mother quietened down. Maybe she wanted to hear my father cry.

And then after a moment or two she said evenly, "I don't want to live like this anymore. I'm fed up, Benny. I'm fed up with your affairs, your lies, your promises. I'm fed up with you. I'm even fed up with *me*."

Then everything was quiet. I heard nothing except the *swoosh-swoosh-swoosh* of the planets on my screen saver orbiting the sun.

"So just go," my mother said softly. "Please just go."

"Lucy," my father began, barely audible. "Let me—"

"I said *go*!" she shrieked. "Go!"

I jerked up. I put my hand on my heart to keep it from crashing through my chest.

I heard Herr Pomplun's three German shepherds next door, barking.

And then I heard my father's footsteps on the parquet floors. They were moving farther and farther away from me.

And then I couldn't hear them anymore.

The front door opened and then closed.

He was gone.

My father was gone.

Papa.

I slowly cracked open my door, expecting to find my mother lying in a desolate heap on the floor in the

187

hall. But she must have crept off without me hearing her.

The apartment was veiled in darkness. Almost spooky. But down the hall I detected a faint light. I followed it to the living room, where I found my mother, sitting in near darkness on the green sofa, staring ahead, comatose-like. She was positioned so far back, her feet barely touched the floor. She looked like a little girl sitting there, helpless and lost. All she needed to complete the picture was a pair of patent leather Maryjanes. She glanced up at me, and for a moment I wanted to sit down next to her and take her in my arms, comfort her. I almost cried, I felt so bad for her.

But then she shifted her weight and she looked like an adult again, like my mother, Lucy Bloom-Edelmeister, woman wonder. And something in me just snapped. A furious white light flashed and I suddenly found myself angry. Really angry.

"It's all your fault," I said to her.

She looked at me. "Maybe," she said. "Maybe."

"He didn't even say goodbye."

"That wasn't my fault."

I began to cry.

"Oh, honey," she said, coming to me.

But before she reached me, before she had the chance to take me in her arms, and I to fall into them, or maybe even spurn them, the doorbell rang. I literally felt the blood rush back to my face. And I'm pretty sure my mother's face got some color back, too. I ran to the front door, my mother at my heels. My father was back!

I swung open the door. And there stood a very fat, very bald, very rosy-cheeked, and very un-Papa-like man.

"Good evening," he said to my mother. "Wilko Kompatzki. Kompatzki Catering. We have an appointment." He looked down at me. "Ah! You must be the happy bat mitzvah girl!"

I survived the night. I think Max was right. The fresh air was good for me. It put me to sleep and kept me there.

I awoke more or less fit and was out of the house before my mother and Risa were up and about. I had to speak to Max. Immediately. Or did he already know about my parents? Had my father spent the night at his house? How *could* he?

But I couldn't find Max on campus. I went inside, where, among all the swarming kids, it was even harder to find him.

"Are you deaf, or what?" someone hollered in my ear.

I swung around. It was Pia. I must've frowned, because she said, "You don't look thrilled to see me."

I shrugged, keeping my eyes on the crowd, on the lookout for Max.

"In fact, you look awful," Pia said, suddenly compassionate. "My God, what happened?"

For a second I thought I was going to cry. Why

189

was she being so nice to me? I just wanted to be left alone so I could find Max.

"Oh, I don't know," I said. "Nothing. My parents. Forget it."

"All right," she said. "So do you have my letter?"

"Somewhere." My hand dove into my backpack and fumbled around impatiently. My pencil case. My wallet. My raspberry lipstick. My pad.

"No, really, what's wrong?" Pia said. "You look so distraught."

I looked up. "Distraught?" I said. "You're using such big words today. And besides, I don't want to talk about it."

The comment didn't go over well. "You know, you can be a real snotnose," Pia snapped.

"I didn't mean it like—"

And then I saw Max.

And something startling happened.

I felt a sudden surge of warmth in my stomach, like a wave, a huge swelling wave. Max smiled at me, and the world as I knew it stopped. Me, Max, and the air between us were the only things that existed. As I walked toward him, he waved and my stomach filled up with warmth again. His eyes seemed to wander behind me. My head moved around in a reflex reaction and I saw Yvonne.

My stomach contracted.

Max was smiling at *Yvonne*! Not at me. He had waved at *her*.

I watched them come together and walk away

happily, talking animatedly like in a television commercial for sugarless chewing gum. Or life insurance.

I was back in the school hallway.

"Uh-oh," Pia said.

"He just didn't see me—that's all."

"I wonder why," Pia said, not without sarcasm.

"Hi," said a voice behind us.

It was Anton. Pia's face lit up like the Rockefeller Center Christmas tree. I wondered for a moment if that's the way I looked when I saw Max.

"I hear you're trying out for the girls' basketball team later," Anton said to me. To *me*.

Since when did Anton Weissenberger talk to *me* in a normal tone of voice?

"Yes, I am," I said. "Later. I'll be trying out later..." My voice trailed off as I watched Max and Yvonne disappear down the hall.

"Where are you going?" Anton asked me. "I'll walk with you."

Pia's rosy cheeks lost their color. Why wasn't Anton offering to walk *her* to class? I didn't need him—that was for sure. My mother, though, would have been thrilled. The rabbi's son was finally accepting my existence. Hallelujah. Ring the bells. Blow the shofar.

"Thanks, I'll be fine," I said to Anton. I pointed to the girls' room. "I guess you can't walk with me in there, can you?" I smiled at him, winked at Pia, and made a beeline for the bathroom.

I thought Pia would follow me in, but she didn't.

I sat down in one of the stalls and was suddenly overcome by a terrible sense of despair. In my mind's eye I saw my father disappearing down the hall, heard his footsteps fade slowly in the distance, saw my mother sitting on the sofa, staring ahead, heard my father shut the door, saw my mother's tears flood her cheeks. I felt a knot swell in my throat and was about to give myself up to it, when the bathroom door opened and then closed.

"Pia?" I said.

"No," I heard someone say in the stall next to mine.

I forced the tears down. I wasn't going to cry with someone in the next stall. Instead, I blew my nose with some toilet paper and willed myself to conjure up an image of Max. And it worked. My stomach got all warm and gooey-like again. I closed my eyes and pictured Max in his tank top. And the rolling waves came back.

What did Max want from Yvonne? Sex? Was it possible that he was interested in her? My stomach knotted up.

I rose. I had to get out of the bathroom. I had to be among people. I had to get through the day. I flushed the toilet and went to the mirror.

I took a quick survey. Pia was right: I looked awful. I straightened my braid, combed my bangs, put on some raspberry lipstick, and dabbed some of it on my cheeks for blush. I *had* to talk to Max. But first I'd give Pia her stupid letter. I found it at the bottom of my backpack and opened the door to the hallway. But Pia was gone. Preoccupied, I slipped the letter in the side pocket of my backpack and made my way down the hall.

I found Max during recess. But he wasn't alone. He was playing soccer with a couple of guys. Some kids, among them Yvonne, Nicole, and Caroline, were hanging out on the other side of the field, shivering in the cold, following the game. I took off my heavy backpack and waited at the sidelines, jumping up and down to keep warm, shuffling my feet, and being generally impatient, hoping Max would look my way, but he didn't. Finally, one of the boys had pity on me and got Max's attention.

"I'm in the middle of a game," he said, running over.

"I know that. But it's urgent."

We walked off a bit to the side, out of eavesdropping range.

"Hey, Max!" one of the boys called out. "Since when do you talk to nerds?"

"Be right there," he said. He turned back to me. His voice was gentle. "How do you feel?"

"I never felt better in my life."

"He stayed over last night, but in the living room, if that's what you want to know. And this morning she kicked him out. I heard her say something like, 'You're not a kid anymore. You have to make a decision.' And then she said, 'I already have

193

one teenager in the house. I don't need two.'"

"Serves him right!" I said. "Do you know that he—" I couldn't get it past my lips.

"What?"

"He—" Oh, my God, was I going to burst out in tears? Right here in front of everybody? "He slept with my mother's best friend!"

Max whistled.

"Her *best* friend!" I said, and took a deep breath to keep myself from crying.

I was surprised at my own anger. But then a second or two later, I felt as if I had betrayed my father, revealed one of his secrets. I could already feel pangs of guilt.

"I think my mother cares for him, Nelly. She let him plow her, didn't she?"

"Do you have to be so explicit?"

Max rolled his eyes. "And I also think he really likes my mother. I don't think it's just an affair."

It was my turn to roll my eyes.

"Maybe she kicked him out because she just doesn't want any problems right now," Max said.

"Don't you think it's a little late for that? I mean, she stole a married man. Of course there were going to be problems."

Max grinned. "She probably thinks your mother will come after her with a ten-ton frying pan."

I tried to conjure up a picture of my mother with a ten-ton frying pan and actually could. I almost laughed. "Well, maybe now he'll come back to us,"

I said, for a moment relieved, almost lighthearted.

"Don't count on it."

"What makes you so sure?"

"I've already been there."

"Hey, Max, are you in or out?" one of the boys called out. "Either you take her behind the bushes or get back in here!"

One of the other boys called out and made kissing noises.

"I'm in!" Max called back. He turned to me and I could tell he was blushing. "Gotta go!"

I frowned. "After the tryouts, then."

He looked down at his sneakers. They were black—like everything else he wore. "I'm busy," he said.

I can't say for sure, but I'm pretty certain he inadvertently looked at Yvonne.

"You're busy?" I said. "Why? What? I thought—"

"Look, Nelly, we're friends, right? But we're not married. I have stuff to do. We had a deal and it's done." He looked at the field. The boys were standing impatiently, waiting for him. "See you," he said, running back to his game.

Right. We had a deal. And it's done. And I didn't even get the sex.

I noticed how gray the skies were. How low the clouds. How raw the wind. Yvonne turned to me, a smirk on her face. Discouraged, I turned to go and practically bumped into Anton.

"Nelly," he said, his face flushed, "I found this.

Over there." He held up the envelope with Pia's letter. "It was on the grass next to your backpack."

Oh, my God! It must have fallen out of the side pocket when I took off the backpack.

"I saw my name on the envelope," Anton was saying, "so I took the liberty of opening it, and … I thought…"

He was stuttering and blushing and hardly the Anton Weissenberger I knew. And me? I wasn't the Nelly he knew, either. I was never so tongue-tied in my entire life. I wanted to disappear through a hole in the ground, a wormhole if need be.

"I'm sorry," I said. "I didn't mean to … I mean … I…"

"I figured it was you," Anton said.

"Oh, no. You don't understand. It's not…"

He patted his butt. "No one except you could have known what 'gluteus muscles' are." He stretched out his arm. "And here, feel my biceps."

"Oh, no. I can't."

"Of course you can."

Out of the corner of my eye, I saw that Max had stopped playing and was looking at us. *I'll show him,* I thought, raising my hand to Anton's arm. As I did so, I was suddenly aware of Pia watching us, too. Embarrassed, I made a movement to pull my hand away, but Anton, quicker, put his other hand on mine and flexed his muscle. I felt the upper arm muscle harden and rise, like in a stupid old Popeye cartoon. Anton smiled down at me.

196

"That's really something," I said to him—but only halfheartedly, because on the other side of the court I saw Max stare at me, then pull off his sweatshirt and drape it over Yvonne's shoulders. A moment later I felt a burning sensation in my stomach, as if it had been slashed with a superfine X-Acto knife.

Things continued to get worse. Just like in a Hollywood movie. Do you know how in the movies, when it rains, it always pours? Just when it looks as if the hero is about to get what he wants, something thwarts him. And that little irritant breeds a problem, and then another problem crops up, and then that leads to a disaster, and then, uh-oh, here comes a major catastrophe, and just when you think nothing worse can happen, because the hero has already suffered through enough, of course something even worse than the major catastrophe occurs: the mega meltdown. Well, that's kind of like how I felt as I walked into the girls' locker room to get dressed for the basketball game. It wasn't enough that my parents wouldn't be there, that my father had left us, that my mother was comatose, that Max had scorned me, Pia was angry at me, and that Anton was after me. The laws of logic told me that things were going to get worse before they got better.

Pia got the ball rolling. I was dressing for the big game, tying my sneakers, when she flew into the locker room, her long, flaming red hair trailing behind her like a flickering candle. "I thought you were my friend," she said, her eyes dark and earnest.

"I *am* your friend," I said evenly.

"You stole Schwarzenegger from me."

I knew she was going to say that. "It just looks like that," I said. "But I didn't. I didn't do anything."

"Were you fondling his muscles or not?"

I found her use of the word *fondling* awkward but opted against bringing it up. It would only make things worse. I felt bad for Pia, but what could I do? What could I say?

"He thinks you wrote the letters," she went on.

"The problem is, I *did*. But you can tell him you wrote them, can't you?"

"I will!" she said.

"Well, make sure you know what gluteus muscles are."

My last remark was not meant to be nasty. I really wanted her to know exactly where the gluteus muscles were. But it came out wrong somehow.

"How *could* you?" she asked. "Why do you always have to make me feel so stupid?"

And she was gone.

Should I run after her, try to patch things up, and be late for the game, possibly even be disqualified? Or should I try to straighten things out later? I chose the latter.

It had been a hard day—perhaps the hardest of my life. Before getting up from the bench, I took stock. What was I, Nelly Sue Edelmeister, age thirteen, 154.5 centimeters tall, 47¾ kilos, 148 IQ, straight-A average, a Westinghouse aspirant and future cosmologist, what was I doing in sneakers and gym shorts and elbow guards? Why was I doing this? How had this madness begun? I wanted to see Prince William, right? I wanted to get to England. Ergo I wanted to get on the basketball team that was going to England. But obviously something had happened along the way that made it more than that. Now I didn't just want to meet Prince William; I wanted to *prove* that I could get on that basketball team, that I could be just like everybody else—prove it to Yvonne & Co., prove it to my mother, to Max.

But it wasn't only that, was it? I also knew that I wanted to prove it to someone else, someone with skinny legs, strong prescription glasses, and a thick head; someone who would never in a million years believe I could do it, someone who's so brilliant, she can't even understand the simplest of passions. In short, I wanted to prove it to *me*. I wanted to prove to myself that I could do it.

And I would.

I was going to dribble my way to fame.

I stood up and took a step. And fell flat on my face. I had tied my shoelaces together.

Two new players were needed for the team. One of them was undoubtedly going to be Tall Tillie. Sixteen other girls were vying to be the other player.

199

You didn't have to be a mathematician to know the odds were against me.

The candidates were seated in the first row of bleachers on the right. On the other side of the bleachers sat the jury. The idea behind the basketball game was this: the existing girls' basketball team was split into two opposing teams of six players each, each side to be supplemented during every quarter by two players from the group of candidates. Each candidate therefore got about fifteen minutes on the floor, and in those fifteen minutes she had to do her damnedest to steal the ball, shoot, score, dribble, pass—anything that would get her points in the eyes of the jury.

I'd never been to one of these tryout games, so I had no idea what to expect. I was surprised to find the gym crowded with kids blowing whistles and cranking up noisemakers, clapping, and shouting with the cheerleaders, who chanted encouraging jingles for the candidates: "Susi Ulrich, Susi Ulrich, go, go, go." Adults were scattered about, too, the parents of candidates and some members of the Parents Association who were selling drinks and snacks. I saw Risa, Frau Goldfarb, and Frau Lewi, but couldn't find Max anywhere. My eyes searched the rows to see if my parents perhaps *had* come, but no, they hadn't. I did notice Pia though, sitting in the first row of bleachers to the side of me.

I was relieved that I wasn't among the first to be called to the floor. I was glad, too, that I wasn't playing with Tall Tillie. She stole the show in the latter part of the first half. But when I wasn't called up after the break, I started getting fidgety. Self-doubt began creeping into my consciousness. I was the only one of the candidates who had taken a basketball with her into the gym. No one else had joined their team by dribbling onto the court. I was sure that when I did, the crowd would boo or maybe the judges would even penalize me for being a showoff. Worse yet: maybe I'd goof up and make a fool of myself. I probably wasn't half as good as I thought. Max had just said so to make me feel good, the way a big brother might say something nice to his kid sister to shut her up. Yes, that was it, I was convinced, and was about to get up and leave when Frau Sander blew her whistle and raised the megaphone. "And now the last four," she announced. "Red team: Karla Schmidt and Yvonne Cohen. Blue team: Nana Seeberger and Nelly Edelmeister."

You see? Didn't I tell you? It was just like I said. My life was like a Hollywood movie, a succession of obstacles upon obstacles upon obstacles. There I was, Nelly Sue Edelmeister, once again pitted against my archenemy, Yvonne Cohen.

Karla, Yvonne, and Nana ran to their respective teams to tremendous applause. I stood up, gulped down some air, jumped over my shadow, and dribbled onto the court. I took a roundabout way, figure-eighting past Pia and then the jury, on past Frau Sander (who was actually staring with her mouth open). I heard loud clapping, and the noisemakers seemed even noisier than they had been before. When I got to the center line, Meredith Hastings, the captain of the red team, grabbed my ball away. The audience booed.

Meredith pushed the ball back into my hands. "Get rid of it," she commanded.

I kicked the ball away and watched it roll toward the bleachers.

"Showoff," Yvonne said under her breath.

My cheeks stung, but I must confess that it was with great pleasure that I heard those words. Max's ploy had worked! Now all I had to do was make sure I didn't make a fool of myself.

When I finally found myself out on the court, I simply wasn't prepared for the fast, violent movement, the heavy breathing, all the sneakers and elbows rushing by. I felt like I had two left feet and no right hand. I stood by helplessly as Yvonne easily got the ball and pushed it upcourt. She took a shot and scored a point.

"T-o-p-s, Yvonne is tops!" the cheerleaders, the Twain Twisters, chanted.

Wild hoots came from the bleachers. Monika Kladow, the captain of my team, yelled over to me to "guard Yvonne, for God's sake!" Now I had to stay between Yvonne and the ball. But I couldn't. Then I had to stay between Yvonne and the basket. And I couldn't, either. Yvonne was dribbling; I was guarding her. Her straight blond hair swayed vigorously to and fro—like a cornfield about to be hit by a tornado. Sweat was forming on my neck under my frizzy braid. It was bouncing on my back, going *thwaap-whuumpp-thwaap-whuumpp* every time I made a sudden movement. I had to get the ball away from her. I had to do some figure eights or I'd never get chosen for the team.

"Come on, four-eyes," Yvonne goaded me on, "try to get the ball away from me. I know you can't. Max said you couldn't."

"No, he didn't. And yes, I can!"

"Yes, he did. And no, you can't. Look, there he is. And he's rooting for me."

I turned, and sure enough, there was Max, sitting with Caroline and Nicole. Miserable, I turned back to the game. But I was too late! Yvonne was already aiming. The ball shot through the air like a cannonball. Oh, I could have hit myself! How lame could I get? Why did I let her distract me? She fooled me with the stupidest trick in the book.

But her shot missed! It bounced off the rim and she moved in to grab the rebound, but I was a nanosecond faster. I shot up and—*pfaff!*—I had the ball.

"Go, Nelly, go!" I heard the Twain Twisters chant. "Go, Nelly, go!"

I had the ball. I finally had it! My fingertips were doing a jig on its rough surface. My feet were moving with it. And Yvonne was close. Perfect. I began my mantra: take the ball in your right hand, spread your legs, put your left leg forward, guide the ball around your right foot... I began dribbling between my legs. My legs, my knees, my whole body was one with the ball. But not my eyes. They were in front of me, looking for someone to pass the ball to. But no one on my team was near me. Where was everybody? I had almost dribbled through a full court all by myself, doing figure eights. I could see the basket. Where was my team? I had to pass the ball. There was no way I could shoot. I'd make such a damn fool of myself!

"Shoot!" I heard the audience scream. "Shoot!"

I aimed. And shot. The ball twirled around the rim once and fell through the hoop.

A basket! I made a basket!

I wanted to scream. Cry. Kiss the heavens. But there was no time for that. The ball was already on its way to the other side of the court. Feet were stamping. Whistles tweeting. Noisemakers squawking. Everything that had been a part of my day—my anger, my jealousy, my sadness—was suddenly consumed by the feverish pace of the game. Nothing mattered anymore, nothing except the ball, the basket, my team.

And so the game went on. Second by second. Minute by minute. Yvonne scored a couple of baskets; my team, though, was two points ahead. I caught the ball twice, made a couple of figure eights, and then passed the ball to another team member. I lost track of time—that's how absorbed I was. I was gone to the world—like when I sat in front of my window and gazed out at the stars. Or like in that dream I had, moving among the stars, exhilarated into flight by the wonder of the universe.

In the end, that one basket of mine was the only one I scored that day, but when Frau Sander blew the whistle, when I saw her incredulous face, when I saw the astonished faces of Risa, Frau Goldfarb, and Frau Lewi, the girls on the team, the audience, Pia, I knew for certain that I'd done it. I had proven to them that I was a winner! Now it was up to the jury to confirm it.

I dressed quickly while the jury deliberated. Back in the gym, I was hoping to find Max. He found me.

"And?" I said.

"You were good," he said.

"Is that all you can say? That I was good? I was terrific!"

Max shrugged. "Considering what you were before, yes."

"I'm going to get on the team! And I'm going to England!"

Max seemed to lose color for a second. "I'm sure Prince William will be very proud of you," he said, not without some sarcasm. He looked at me as if he were waiting for me to say something. "And?"

"And what?"

"Ever hear of the words 'thank you'?" he asked. "T-h-a-n-k y—"

"I know how to spell it, Max."

"I was just wondering if you also know how to *say* it, that's all." He about-faced.

I was, admittedly, embarrassed. How could I have forgotten a simple thank-you?

"Wait a sec," I said.

Max whipped around, lashing out at me with a "What!"

I had wanted to apologize, but his anger hurt me. Or was it the sudden knowledge that he wasn't wearing his sweatshirt that upset me so? I looked toward the bleachers and saw Yvonne there, his sweatshirt adorning her shoulders.

"You were the one who said we had a deal and it was done," I lashed out angrily. "Do I have to say thank you for the rest of my life?" I was close to tears. "I've had a really hard day, and a really hard night. I thought you at least would be a bit more understanding."

Someone blew a whistle and we saw the jury was returning. Fearing I'd break out in tears right in front of Max, I ran to Risa.

The ladies made a fuss over me, praising and hugging and kissing. Risa, a bit more reserved than usual, merely took my hand and patted it. Frau Lewi offered me some popcorn and I almost choked on it. Frau Goldfarb pinched my cheek. Her Parkinson fingers were so trembly, the pinch felt like a massage. It was nice being with the "girls," but I think I would have been happier if my mother and father had been there, too.

The loudspeaker exploded with static. "It wasn't easy coming to a decision this afternoon," Frau Sander said. "We'd like to thank all of the girls who tried out today, thank them for their dedication and their hard work." She looked at me. Straight at *me*. "Some of you did an astonishingly good job! And I want you to know that if you didn't make the team today, please try out again next season." She looked down at a note she was holding. "Okay. This is the moment you've all been waiting for. The two new members of the Twain Tigresses are ..." She paused and then, like a presenter on the Academy Awards show, she emceed "... Mathilda Lichtenberg and Yvonne Priscilla Cohen."

Tall Tillie and Yvonne ran to the center of the court, all smiles and waves and bows. I fell against Risa and she took me in her arms. Her glass stone poked me in the chest, and I smelled her perfume, *Je reviens*.

"Bubeleh, you tried your best and that's what counts," Risa said to me.

"I failed," I said. "*That's* what counts."

"I'm hungry," said Frau Lewi. "And *that,* my dear ladies, is what *really* counts." She raised her hand to catch our waitress's attention, but the waitress was wearing blinders, or so it seemed.

It was crowded in Tanzcafé Tietze. Risa went there with her friends whenever they got nostalgic for the music of their youth: the Comedian

207

Harmonists, *Die drei Rulands,* Marlene Dietrich, Count Basie, *"Ich küsse Ihre Hand, Madam."* A bunch of seniors were on the dance floor perfecting a waltz. The music was terribly old-fashioned and the recordings crackled with static, but you could tell that the recording artists were having fun — more than I can say for my mood that evening.

"Nelly," Risa said, "why concern yourself with success or failure? That all depends on things beyond your control. Who's to say why the jury didn't choose you? They probably don't know themselves. Just think what a miracle it is that you accomplished something that only a few weeks ago you would never have dreamed possible."

I was tired of listening to Risa. She reminded me of my father. Who had my mother called him? Kahlil Gibran? I'd have to look that name up.

"Nelly, *Schätzchen,*" Frau Goldfarb said, "come boogie with me."

I declined. Out of the corner of my eye, I could see the three women exchange looks, and I was suddenly aware that they knew all about last night and my parents.

"Did my father call or anything?" I asked Risa.

I could tell that Risa didn't like the question. I suppose she didn't want to be put on the spot. She shrugged and said, "Well, if you won't boogie, I will." She bopped to the dance floor with Rosi Goldfarb.

It was arguably the worst day of my life, but I

remember nonetheless being fascinated by Risa and Frau Goldfarb. A tango was on, "Hernando's Hideaway." Their dance steps seemed so intricate — especially on Frau Goldfarb's high-heeled feet. I remember wondering where they had ever learned to dance like that. At a dancing school? Before the war? Postwar? And what a miracle it was that after all they'd been through, they still remembered how to do it.

The tango faded into a foxtrot. And a couple of minutes later, a jitterbug came on. I sat there watching, yet not watching, playing the basketball game over and over again in my head. And when it began to bore me, I went about winding and rewinding in my head a tape of my parents' fight. And when I got tired of that, I watched another program in my mind's eye: Max draping his sweatshirt over Yvonne's shoulders. And when that image was too painful, I changed the channel and saw Pia's indignant facial expression.

Laughter and the sound of clapping brought me back to the dance café. The whole room was having a rollicking time. The women were singing along to "Rum and Coca-Cola," bouncing their heads from side to side coquettishly. But then, amid the racket, I faintly heard Frau Lewi gasp. I followed her eyes to the dance floor.

Some people remember the smell of the hospital most, that antiseptic, squeaky-clean odor that sears

209

your nose the moment you enter the building. Or the color of the walls—yellow, beige, sometimes mint green. Some say it's the rhythmic *plop-plop-plop* of the intravenous that sticks in their minds. Or the ugly institutional furniture.

I remember the *squish-squash* sound of the doctor's shoes as he came toward us with news of Risa. One second she was dancing; the next she had collapsed on the floor. And now, two hours later, an emergency room doctor was *squish-squashing* his way over to us to tell us whether Risa was alive. Or maybe dying. Perhaps already dead.

"Frau Edelmeister?" the doctor said. He was wearing a stethoscope with a miniature stuffed panda hanging on it, and a pen was dangling precariously from his breast pocket. His face was earnest.

My mother stood up. "Yes?"

He smiled. "I'm Dr. Leuchtmann. We'd like to keep Frau Ginsberg here until tomorrow noon. Sometimes a minor heart event like this is a foreboding for a major attack."

A minor heart event? *Minor?* My heart exploded majorly, rejoicing so suddenly as it did.

"So she'll be okay?" my mother said.

The doctor smiled reassuringly. "She looks pretty strong to me."

Risa was propped up in her bed when I entered her room. I took in the darkness and fuzzy forms, the room illuminated solely by a small lamp on Risa's night table. I was expecting to find a state-of-the-art hospital environment with high-tech equipment, electronic graphs looping up and down, beeps representing heartbeats beeping on and off, plastic water-bag-like containers hanging upside down from metal stands with tubes. But all I saw was tiny little Risa in a blue hospital nightgown dozing, or perhaps daydreaming, in bed. No intravenous, no tubes in her nose, no catheter, no nothing. She really *was* going to be all right!

The door clicked shut behind me, and Risa turned to me. She smiled and I went to her, plunking down on the chair next to her bed.

"We were so worried about you!" I said.

She looked reasonably puzzled. "Worried? About me?"

Was it possible that she was unaware of the seriousness of her attack? I stared at her. "Yes, you!"

"Me?" she asked with such exaggerated astonishment I knew she was pulling my leg. But her theatrics seemed to ooze the strength out of her, because she closed her eyes and leaned back against the pillow. I noticed that she was holding her glass stone in her hand, rubbing it, fondling it, the way I saw old Greek men play with their rosaries when I was with my parents on Crete one summer.

"Mom said I can talk to you for two minutes and then I have to go home," I said.

She opened her eyes and smiled. "Smart lady. It's late."

"She said she'll stay with you after."

Risa nodded and I was aware that she was short of breath.

"What did it feel like?" I ventured to ask.

"It was a pain, bubeleh. But I've had worse."

She wasn't in the mood to talk about it—the way she never wanted to talk about the war. She propped herself up. "Let me hug you," she said.

I couldn't sleep that night. I sat on my armchair looking out at the heavens, watching clouds floating in and out, an airplane and a helicopter gliding across my window, moist with rain, the smeared yellow window rectangles a few blocks away blinking on and off. Below me was the midnight blackness of the deserted garden plots; above me, the skies veiled in rain clouds. I watched the moon bobbing in and out of the clouds like a big fat buoy in a mean old sea. I watched my clock move its hands around and around and around. I watched birds fluttering away in a commotion, frightened out of sleep by the sudden sound of shattering glass.

And then all was quiet again.

For a long time there was only stillness.

Then I felt a chill. I turned to my door and realized that my mother was in the room. She was wearing her trench coat, dripping with rain, her boots muddy. The ceiling light from the hallway behind her shone down on her head so that her hair, sparkly with wet, frizzy, and sticking up, looked like a corona. What was she doing here? Why wasn't she in the hospital?

She came to me and knelt on the floor. She took my hands.

My mother's mouth twisted up, and then down, and for a second she looked like those masks that portray comedy and tragedy, a face with a huge cutout smile and a face with a gross frown. She moaned and big fat tears started rolling down her cheeks. I watched them plop down along her nose, get all over her mouth, run along her chin, and then drop to her chest.

I felt panic.

"I was sitting there, Nelly, talking to her," said my mother. "And then she closed her eyes. I didn't think anything of it. Why shouldn't she close them? But then she was so still. And I realized that she was too still." My mother closed her eyes a moment to watch the movie in her head. Then she looked at me. "It was her heart," she said. "It just stopped. It stopped, and she was gone."

My mother dropped her head to my lap. It felt heavy. Like a hundred-pound bowling ball. She clasped her arms around my waist. I couldn't breathe. I reached behind me and tried to gently take her hands away, but they stuck to me like leeches.

"I'm so sorry, honey," she said. "I'm so sorry."

My ears started to buzz. And then they plugged up. And then buzzed again. It scared me. I felt the palms of my hands get all sweaty. I could smell my mother's hair, the sickly sweetness of her shampoo. And it made be nauseous. She was rocking back and forth, and her trench coat, the poplin, made a deafening sound as it rubbed against my lap.

I yanked my mother's hands away. She looked up, surprised.

"Now everybody's gone," I said. "Everybody. Risa. And Papa. Max. Pia. Everybody. Everything. Now I don't have anyone."

I started to cry.

My mother reached out to take me in her arms, to stroke my forehead, caress my hair, I don't know exactly what. "Nelly, honey, my little baby," she said. "*I'm* here."

I pulled away. "You? I don't want you. I want Papa. I want Risa."

I flung myself on my bed.

And then the black hole sucked me in.

11

The Big Chill

Risa was buried within a day, but she'd have to wait a year before she got a gravestone. Jewish law says that as long as the Kaddish, the prayer for the dead, is being said—and that's for an entire year—the deceased remain alive in our memories and don't need a gravestone. I wished she had one though, as some sort of protection against the elements. When I went to visit her in the cemetery, and I went practically every day that first week, it hurt to watch the wind and rain pounding down mercilessly on the soft earth where she had disappeared just a few days before.

One afternoon I decided to gather fallen leaves and spread them on her gravesite like a blanket. I knew it was a ridiculous idea. Risa was gone from me forever, with or without leaves for protection, but creating a warm blanket of autumnal leaves for her was a welcome distraction.

My father and I spent time with each other every few days or so those first weeks. My mother and father saw each other as well. At first I thought that they had mended things, since I never heard them raise their voices anymore. But at the end of the evening my father always left, or if they met outside the apartment, my mother came home alone. My father was staying just a few blocks away, with his Australian friend, Grant Neville, the bass player. Apparently Grant was moving to England early next year. If my father was able to find a steady job, it looked like he might be taking over Grant's apartment. The thought upset me. I missed us being a threesome together, being mommy and daddy and little me. A new apartment for my father would make a reconciliation unlikely. I tried not to think about it.

The constant stream of guests and mourners during the first week after Risa's death helped keep me busy. Max actually came by once to pay his respects. My mother was surprisingly civil to him and even offered him her last four rugelach cookies. Frau Pinto, a friend of Risa's, had baked them. My mother had stashed away the last remaining ones in the hope of devouring them herself once the visitors that day were gone—until Max arrived. Max gladly took them and sat down next to me on the green suede sofa.

Max made an effort to start a conversation, but we had nothing to say to each other, or rather, we had too *much* to say and it left us speechless. I was disappointed in him for not understanding my predicament the day of the game. He was disappointed in me for being ungrateful. I had this image in my head of him draping his Stuyvesant sweatshirt over Yvonne's shoulders, and he of me "flirting" with Anton. At least that's how I see it now with hindsight. In any case, we were stubborn enough not to talk to each other.

Religious Jews actively mourn the dead for seven days. Sitting shivah is quite a complicated affair, with a variety of rituals that go back thousands of years—everything from sitting on pillows instead of on chairs, covering all the mirrors in the house, not showering or bathing, and not wearing shoes with leather soles. We didn't do any of that— thank God. Imagine giving up showers for a whole week! But my mother did keep a candle lit for seven days. She explained that just in case there *is* some sort of Beyond—and after all, who was she to say there wasn't?—the flickering flame might help Risa's ascent.

Occasionally I sat at my mammoth window and tried to find some sign of Risa up there in the sky, or even just a patch of light in the darkness, but when I looked outside all I saw were dark clouds and the coming of a tediously long winter. I remembered Risa telling me and Max that light is everywhere, even in darkness. That we just have to find it. And if we set our hearts to it, we can learn to reflect it. I stared and stared at the black skies and wondered where Risa had ever found the strength to do that. I felt I had failed her, especially since I had called off the bat mitzvah the day after her death. With her gone, the bat mitzvah seemed a meaningless gesture. Nonetheless, I wondered if she knew about my decision and if it disturbed her. I cried terribly when it hit me that I'd never be able to ask her.

One night, while staring out at the emptiness, I heard something knocking softly on my window. It was a bug, big and brownish and ugly, about two inches long and a half inch wide. It looked like a giant cricket, but I wondered if crickets could fly four flights up, or even fly. I'm not a big fan of insects, crickets or otherwise, so I tried to shoo it away by tapping on the window. But the bug was insistent. It just kept on banging its body against the pane as if it wanted to come in. It occurred to me that maybe the bug needed to tell me something. I wondered if it had some kind of message from Risa. Maybe it was even Risa herself. Against my better judgment, I opened the window to let it in. To my relief, it stayed outside, staring, staring, keeping sentinel outside in the cold throughout the night.

When I awoke in the morning, it was still there, but when I came back from school, I was devastated to find that it was gone. The whole incident left me feeling so strangely abandoned. But then I went into Risa's room and sprayed her room a couple of times with her *Je reviens* perfume, sniffing it and moving around in it until for a fleeting moment I had the feeling that Risa was, indeed, back home.

But it was only for a moment.

Outside, the leaves fell, and inside, even my own room felt empty and gray. Bubbe, my computer, sat alone and forgotten on my desk; the illustration of the Vixen telescope, hanging next to my mirror, seemed to mock me; and Prince William smiled vacuously at me from his home in the closet. For the past week he'd been out of my thoughts and dreams. I realized I hadn't looked at his poster for days. I tried to see the grief of loss in his eyes, but realized the photograph had been taken before his mother's death, of course.

My mother and I rarely spoke to one another, and when we did, it was monosyllabic: how do you want your egg? Soft. What time will you be home this evening? Late. Did you at least write Uncle Bruce about why you called off the bat mitzvah? No. Can I have some money for new gym socks? Yes.

In all fairness to my mother, it was not her fault that we did not get along. I was the one who clammed up when she tried to communicate, or walked out of the room in the middle of her sentence, or said something so snotty and so fresh, I'm surprised she didn't slaughter me right there in the kitchen.

Instead, she retreated to her bedroom. She shut all the windows and curtains, woke late, read her old *New Yorker* magazines during the day, complained of migraines, went to bed early.

Our apartment was dark and cold.

One day, just before school, my mother knocked on my door. She was holding a package.

"I found this cleaning out Risa's room," she said. "It's for Max."

"Max?"

"His suit. Risa apparently finished it."

"What suit?"

"For the opening. It's on Saturday."

I'd completely forgotten. Saturday was October 25—originally the date set for my bat mitzvah, and also the opening of Minsky's deli.

"Do you want to give it to him?" my mother asked.

My answer came without a moment's hesitation. "No."

She arched a brow. "All right. Then I'll mail it." She made a slight movement as if to go, but then something stopped her. Her voice softened. "What happened?"

I didn't want her pity. "What the hell do you care what happened?" I said, surprising even myself with my vehemence. "You never liked him anyway. You should be thrilled we're not friends." I went back to dressing.

"So I suppose you're not going to Minsky's on Saturday."

"No. Are you?" I said.

"No."

"Well, well." I smiled. "Don't we have a lot in common?"

In school, thank goodness, things were working out better than at home. I had become a celebrated personality: Nelly van Exelmeister. But just to keep the record straight, I was not a brilliant athlete. Once I figured out how to play without doing figure eights, I was decent but not spectacular. Nonetheless, considering what I had been before Max's coaching, my improvement—physically as well as socially—was mind-boggling. The elementary school kids stood in awe of me; the high schoolers invited me to join in on their volleyball game and explain the laws of gravity to them. Anton followed me around like Mary's little lamb. Even Yvonne had changed her tune. In her favor, she did not pretend to be my best friend. She was polite, but not overly friendly, and most recently dating Danny Diller, the theater club ace. Had she given up on Max? He on her? Or what? I'd probably never know, I thought, for I wasn't on speaking terms with the two people who might reveal the answer: Pia, my ex-friend, and Max himself, my ex-coach. In fact, they were the only ones in school who seemed thoroughly immune to my new popularity. They remained aloof—or at least that's how it seemed to me.

One afternoon, though, a chance encounter changed things radically—at least with Pia. I had stayed in school late and done my homework in the library. On my way out, I happened to pass a room with a sign on the door that read, ASTRONOMY CLUB—*Today at Five—Here—Come Join Us!* Since when did our school have an astronomy club? It was ten minutes to five. I opened the door and walked in.

The room was empty, but to my sheer astonishment, in its center was the Vixen telescope from Astro*Fritz, set up and just waiting to be put in focus. As I approached the lens, I heard a voice. "She's a beauty, isn't she?"

It was Pia.

A beauty? What did Pia know about beautiful telescopes?

"And she's got all the necessary extras," Pia said. "Even a T-2 ring adapter."

Too much information was coming at me too fast. My brain would normally be able to comprehend a situation such as this quickly enough, but Pia and my Vixen seemed so incompatible a pair, it took me a moment to adjust.

"How did my telescope get here?" I managed to ask.

"What do you mean *your* telescope? It's ours."

"Who's ours?"

"The astronomy club's," she said as if talking to a moron.

"Whose astronomy club?"

"The school's!"

"Since when does the school have an astronomy club?"

222

"Since today. I'm the president. And as president, I got the science department to invest in equipment." She patted the telescope like a pet dog.

"You? You're interested in astronomy?"

"Well, excuse me for having a head on my shoulders," she said defensively.

It was too much for me. "Since when?"

"Since when do I have a head on my shoulders?"

"Since when are you interested in the stars?"

"Since you lent me the book about black holes."

"I had no idea."

"That's because you never asked, you arrogant little snotnose. You took it for granted that I was a bimbo."

Amazing, I thought. It's perfectly amazing. Why hadn't I known? What had kept me from seeing this? Pia was incredible!

"For the smartest girl in the class," Pia said, "you're pretty stupid."

Were she and Max in cahoots? Didn't he say something like that to me, too?

"You're a blockhead," Pia said. "But still I missed you."

"Even though I stole Schwarzenegger away from you?"

She made a face. "You didn't steal him away from me."

"Oh?"

"How could you steal him away from me if I never

223

had him in the first place?"

I smiled. "I missed you, too."

"So are we friends again?" she asked.

"I guess so."

"Good, because the astronomy club needs a vice president."

My heart raced home faster than my feet. For the first time in centuries, ages, eons, I felt something close to joy. I was vice president of the astronomy club! Pia and I were friends again! I burst into my building, almost squashing Herr Pomplun's German shepherds behind the heavy entrance door when I swung it open. I rushed up the four flights two steps at a time. I sprinted through the apartment, looking for my mother.

"I'm home, Mom," I called out. "Mom? ... Mom?" Her office door was closed. I ripped it open. "Mom?"

"Oh!" my mother gasped.

The room was dark. The blinds were shut. She'd been napping on her sofa. She sat up.

"My God, Nelly!" she snapped. "You scared me. I was sleeping!"

"Sorry."

She made a face. "Augh. I have a terrible headache." She rubbed her forehead. "Well, what is it? What's so important?"

"Nothing," I said. "Absolutely nothing."

* * *

My mother was sitting in front of the television, zapping listlessly from channel to channel, sipping on raspberry schnapps when I went in to say good night. The second she was aware of my presence, she clicked the power off, put the remote down, and turned to me. I knew she had something on her mind. I didn't want to know what it was.

"Nelly, can we talk?" she began.

"I'm tired, Mom."

"I am, too," she said, which was tantamount to saying I'd better sit down and pay attention.

I plunked down in the armchair opposite her. "And?"

She didn't like my "and," but decided to ignore it. She inhaled and exhaled deeply. "I was wondering if you might be happier with your father."

My whole face stung, as if she had whacked me with a giant fly swatter. "What's that supposed to mean?" I said, aware of a knot growing in my throat.

"Perhaps you and I are just not good for each other during this stage in our lives." Boy oh boy, was she choosing her words carefully. "It might be better if—"

"Are you trying to get rid of me?" I blurted out. "Is that it?"

"Oh, Nelly! Of course not!"

"Then what is it? Because that's what it sounds like to me." The knot in my throat had grown the size of a golf ball. It was threatening to choke me. "Am I too difficult for you to handle? You don't want any problems? You don't want any headaches? Is that it?"

"You're being unfair!" she said, angry, hurt.

"*I'm* being unfair?"

"What do you take me for, Nelly? Do you really think I enjoy saying 'go to your father'? Do you really think I *want* you to leave me? But I sit here and look at you, see how unsatisfied you are, how unhappy, and I just don't know what to do." She was wringing her hands, struggling with something. Her eyes were looking inside her. When she spoke again it was a whisper. "You know as well as I do that you've always preferred your father to me."

The golf ball dissolved into tears. "That's because he doesn't control me the way you do! That's because he never forces me to be what I'm not! That's because he accepts me the way I am! But you, you never say anything positive. About me. Or anyone. You're always negative."

"Nelly, that's not true!"

"Everything I do is wrong. I always have to be what *you* want and do what *you* want. But I don't want to be *you*, Mom. I just want to be me! Me!"

My mother was crying now, too. "I only want you to be happy."

I sprang up. All my hurt came out at once. And all my meanness, too. "Oh, all of a sudden you really care about how I feel. 'I was wondering if you might be happier with your father.' Ha! Well, you can pretend you care about me as much as you want to. But I don't believe it. None of it! Not for a second. Because all you care about is *you* and what people think about you, and your work, and your success. Period."

I might as well have whipped her. That's how defeated she looked.

"You weren't always like this," she said, her lips quivering. "There was a time when you were a perfectly normal, happy kid. That's all I ever wanted."

"Me, too. That's all I ever wanted, too. All I ever wanted was a perfectly normal, happy mother."

She got up and left the room.

If she had stayed a fraction of a second longer, she might have seen the regret in my eyes. But she was gone. And the distance between us suddenly seemed a million light-years.

I awoke late, racked by questions. Why was my mother trying to get rid of me? Was it because I was a constant reminder of her failure? Did I look too much like my father? Or was she just sick of my moods? I lay in bed wondering if we'd ever be able to get along. Should I stay with her or go to my father? I never needed Risa more than I did that morning. She would have helped me make a decision. Now all I had was me.

I shuffled through the apartment in my slippers and bathrobe looking for my mother, but she was still sleeping. I decided to cut my morning classes and confer with my father.

My father and I met at an outdoor café. We sat watching the morning shoppers walk by, mommies pushing their toddlers in strollers, shopkeepers hauling their wares out to the sidewalk on racks. Across the street a greengrocer set up a Halloween display with pumpkins carved into grotesque faces. My father looked a little haggard himself, but I noticed that the women who passed by smiled at him like in the old days when I was a little girl. I think my father noticed it, too.

"So?" I said. "What do you think?"

"You're welcome to move in with me, princess. It's your decision."

I nodded, relieved. I liked the idea of living alone with my father, that is, as long as we were really alone. Another woman in the house, even someone like Melissa, was utterly unthinkable. I didn't want a stranger hogging the bathroom. Or taking over the kitchen. "I'll cook for you," I said to my father. "I'll iron your shirts."

My father chuckled. "It's the other way around, princess. *I'm* supposed to cook for *you*." He took a sip of his coffee. "But whatever you decide, don't base it on the premise that your mother loves you less than I do."

"But it was *her* idea. First she kicks you out. Then me."

"She's not kicking you out!" he snapped at me. "And besides, one thing has nothing to do with the other."

We were interrupted by a flurry of activity. It was the waitress. "Here you go," she said, putting our breakfast down on the table.

We sat quietly, waiting for her to leave, although I didn't mind the interruption. I needed it to recover from my father's outburst.

The second after the waitress left with a *"Guten Appetit!"* my father dove back into the conversation. "Your mother has her reasons for being angry at me."

"But you're still the best father in the world!" I said.

"Oh, Nelly, Nelly," he said, shaking his head. Then he took my head in his hands and stroked my cheek softly. "Sometimes I love you so much, it hurts." He kissed my forehead and looked at me square in the eyes. "I was a lousy husband, princess. I think you know that."

I looked down, embarrassed.

"But I want you to know that I've given up women," he said with exaggerated earnestness, almost self-mockingly. "All of them. Except, of course, for you."

I looked back up and saw him grinning at me.

"And what about Melissa?" I asked.

The grin was gone immediately. And there he was, blanching. My tone had been harsh. Perhaps I had sounded like my mother.

"We're putting that on hold, princess," he said, "until we figure everything out. I'm just working for her now. That's all."

"Does Mom know?"

"She does. But it doesn't change anything." He was trying to figure out what to say next, but it took a moment for him to get it straight in his head. "I guess it's time for me to wake up, huh?" he said. He smiled, but it got all twisted and for a second I thought he was going to cry. He looked away and I suddenly felt so sad and embarrassed for him.

We didn't talk for a couple of minutes. But then the waitress came and asked if he wanted more coffee and he said yes, and then he steered the conversation back to me and my mother.

"Believe me, she's not getting rid of you," he said. "She just thinks you'd be happier with me. God knows why. You two have your problems, but you need her. She's your mother. And she needs *you*."

"Right! She needs someone to boss around."

"Nelly, she needs you because you're her family. And because she loves you." He sounded annoyed again. He took his index finger and tapped my head with it a couple of times. "When are you going to get that through your thick skull? You're all she's got. You're her everything. Her past. Her future. You're the reason she's here."

"The reason she's here? What's *that* supposed to mean?"

My father took a bite of his croissant, chewed it carefully, sipped his coffee, wiped his lips — all just to buy a minute of thought.

"I'm not so sure that your mother's happy here," he began. "Berlin's not her home. She didn't grow up in this culture. It's not really where her heart ..." His voice trailed off for a moment, while he tried to find the right words. "... sings. Berlin's not where her heart sings and laughs. Where it thrives. Sure, she likes Berlin and she feels at home here. But feeling *at* home is not the same as *being* home, being in that one place where with absolute certainty you know you belong, no questions asked."

"So why'd she stay in the first place?"

"She was in love."

I must have looked a little puzzled, because he felt compelled to add, "With me, princess. She was in love with *me*." He smiled sadly. "And I disappointed her."

"And you think the only thing that keeps her here now is me?"

"Yep."

It was a lot for me to take in.

"And I also think," he added, "it's the reason she stayed married to me so long."

I sat there, nibbling on my roll and looking at the people around me. We didn't say anything for a while. The sun went behind some clouds and it suddenly looked like it might rain.

Two women—maybe they were students; they didn't look much older than in their early twenties—sat down at the table next to us. One of

231

them was extremely tall and skinny with bitterly short and spiky red hair. It was so red, it looked fake. And the other woman was shorter and rounder, but very pretty. She had alabaster-white skin, very smooth and translucent, long, glossy, black hair, a pointed chin, and her lips were perfectly shaped, like a Betty Boop doll, and even more perfectly made up. They were thinly outlined with a dark red lipstick pencil and filled in with a paler shade of red.

"So you think Mom misses America?" I said.

"I think so. Maybe *she* doesn't know it. But *we* do," he said, winking at me.

I gestured toward the fruit and vegetable shop across the street. The greengrocer was looking up at the sky, wondering if it was going to rain.

"Maybe I should bake her a pumpkin pie for Halloween," I said.

He grinned. "You and your mother are more alike than you realize, princess. You've got a good sense of humor. And you're sharp. Just like her."

I noticed that the alabaster-skinned woman had unbuttoned her blazer, although the sun was gone. Underneath was a low-cut, burgundy sweater. She was talking to her girlfriend, but at the same time stealing glances at my father and running her fingers through her hair. Her nail polish was the same color as her lipstick. My father caught her eye and she subtly threw her head back, shook her hair, and then whisked it behind her shoulders, revealing her long, very long neckline. I saw my father smile at her.

I blushed.

"Do you think that's why she goes to synagogue?" I asked my father.

Startled, he turned back to me. "What?"

I had just remembered something Risa said to me a few weeks before that, about how it was important for me to go through with my bat mitzvah because even if I wandered away from religion, which I was sure to do, at least I would always know where home was.

"Do you think that's why Mom goes to synagogue? Even though she's not religious? Because it's like home to her?" I asked my father.

"I never thought of it like that. But maybe." He wondered about it a second. "Yes. I think you might have something there, princess. Yes."

I suddenly had a fluttery feeling in my stomach. As if I were about to discover something of astonishing importance. Like the first time I saw the moon close up using a telescope in the observatory. I felt a rush of excitement as a thought took shape in my head. My words came out slowly, barely above a whisper. "Maybe *that's* why it was so important to her that I have a bat mitzvah. As if through my bat mitzvah I were giving her a link to some kind of home, some spiritual home. What do you think, Papa?"

My father didn't think anything. He wasn't even listening. He was leaning toward the alabaster-

233

skinned woman, close enough to look down her sweater if he wanted to. In fact, I think he was. In any case, he was pointing to something on her open menu.

"Try their fruit and yogurt special," he said.

Alabaster smiled at him. Red put a cigarette in her mouth and my father reached for her lighter and lit the cigarette for her.

I stood up abruptly. "Papa."

He turned to me.

"I'm going."

It seemed like something I should have known all along. And probably did. Because when it finally entered my realm of consciousness that my father really *was* a lousy husband, perhaps even an incorrigibly unfaithful human being, the knowledge didn't come as a surprise, nor did it upset me greatly. I think I always knew it, even if I never allowed myself to think it. So I was sad, yes, but not distraught.

On the train it struck me that in a way it was good that my father wasn't a famous musician. Imagine if the whole world knew about his infidelities. I'd just die of shame. Was that how William felt about his parents and their affairs? It must've been awful for him. I wondered if he was strong enough to stave off the onslaught of gossip without shutting down his heart. If he was strong enough to be himself no matter what his parents were. Perhaps surviving such a trauma would *make* him strong? The past few weeks I'd been estranged from William, but now I felt close to him. Like a good friend.

When I got to Risa's gravesite, the sun was out again. I was surprised to see that not only were the leaves still lying on the earth where I had spread them, but someone had gathered some stones and placed them on top as if to hold them down as you would a flimsy blanket on a windy beach. I stood there for a long, long time, just feeling the wind bite my nose, the warmth of the sun on my cheeks, watching the clouds puff-puffing across the flat blue sky, listening to the rustling of the leaves.

I found my mother in Risa's room amid moving crates. The curtains were shut. She looked up.

"I want to take some of this stuff down to the basement," she said. She smiled and I could tell she was glad to see me. "No school?" she asked.

"I met Papa," I said.

She nodded gravely.

My blue bat mitzvah dress was hanging on Risa's dummy. I reached for one of the sleeves and rubbed the soft velvet absent-mindedly between my fingers. "I was thinking about what you said last night."

"Look, Nelly," she began, "just forget what I—"

"I can live with Papa," I said, interrupting her.

My mother took in a sharp breath. And then lowered herself to Risa's sofa. She smiled, but I think she was just trying to be brave. Obviously she was disappointed. "Fine, honey," she said. "That's probably best."

"I can live with him," I said, "*if* you're on vacation or something. For a couple of weeks. But otherwise, I think you're stuck with me. At least until I grow up."

My mother's mouth dropped open like in the movies when a character is suddenly overwhelmed by surprise.

"So if you need to go to New York to do research on your book, or just to breathe it in because you're homesick, I think I'll be fine with Papa," I said. "At least I *think* I will."

My mother's eyes brimmed over with tears. If I'd known she'd be so emotional about this, I would've sent her an e-mail instead.

I went to the sofa and she took me in her arms. "Nelly, Nelly. My little baby." She kissed me on my head, on my hair. Even on my ear. "Oh, I love you so much. My little baby." She was hugging me very hard, so hard, I could barely breathe. And I didn't care. It felt good being hugged like that. At least for a couple a minutes. But after a while, I have to admit, I needed some air.

"It's stuffy in here," I said. I ripped open the curtains. Dazzling golden light filled the room. I opened up a window and let in the cool autumn air. The sun shone on the dressmaker's dummy, illuminating my bat mitzvah gown.

"Another thing, Mom," I said.

She looked up.

"I want to do the bat mitzvah."

My mother's mouth dropped open—again.

"I've been thinking about what Risa said to me. About how celebrating my bat mitzvah means that I'll always know where home is, my spiritual home. And it makes sense to me."

My mother was still just staring.

"So let's do the bat mitzvah," I went on. "Just like we planned. This Saturday. The twenty-fifth. Otherwise I'd have to learn a whole new Torah portion."

"This Saturday?" she managed to say. "Your bat mitzvah?"

"Look! I know all the Hebrew by heart. I know my Torah portion. I know the haftarah. I can do it."

"But Nelly—"

"But Nelly what?"

She was stunned, trying to figure it all out as fast as she could. "I don't know if the rabbi will want to."

"The rabbi? Don't worry about the rabbi. It's not like he can afford to say no. I mean, they need everyone they can get, right?"

"But—"

"Now what?" I said, rolling my eyes theatrically.

"What about our guests from America?"

"I don't know. I mean, it would be nice to have them, I guess. On the other hand, I'm doing this for *me,* for *us*."

"And where will we celebrate? I canceled the banquet hall."

I hadn't given this question any thought. In fact, I hadn't given *any* of this much thought. But my answer came immediately, as if I had always known it. "We'll do it at Minsky's."

My mother was shocked. "At Minsky's? On Saturday? At their opening?"

"Why not? Everyone will be there anyway. And Melissa will be thrilled to have our guests. It's good for business."

"That's ridiculous, Nelly. I won't set foot in that woman's restaurant."

"Why not? The two of you are allies now."

My mother looked at me, startled.

"Papa told me," I said softly, carefully, "that they're putting it on hold."

My mother rolled her eyes. "Were those *his* words?"

I nodded.

"First of all," she said, "I'm not sure if that's true. And second of all, even if it were, it doesn't make Melissa and me allies. And on top of that, don't make Papa out to be my enemy. I love him. I just can't live with him anymore."

I was grasping at straws. "It's just that ... I don't know ... I just wish we could have a happy ending —that's all."

"Oh, Nelly," she said, breaking out in a smile. "You are so American! A happy ending? My little girl wants a happy ending?" She hugged me. And when she let go, she said, "I'll give it some thought. Maybe."

I couldn't believe my ears. "Really?"

"Maybe."

"And just think," I said, getting excited all over again. "All the food and drinks will already be there. You won't even have to pay for catering."

"Really?" she asked. "That's how little you know. She may not want your father, honey, but I'm sure she'll take our money."

And then, suddenly, a shadow crossed her face. She fell down on Risa's armchair in a swoon. "Oh, no," she cried out. "Oh, no!"

"What's wrong?"

"How can we have a bat mitzvah?" she moaned. "What will I wear? I have nothing to wear!"

Was she serious, or what? For a moment I wasn't sure. But then, to my relief, I watched her pop up and fall into a fit of laughter. I couldn't help but join in, and we laughed and laughed, on and on, and didn't stop, couldn't stop, until we were forced to catch our breath, for if not, we'd simply die of silliness.

"Whoa!" my mother managed to say. "Enough!" She stood up. "Let's get this stuff to the basement."

It was dark in the cellar. It smelled moist and fetid and unhealthy. We walked quickly to our storage area and deposited the boxes fast. Just as we were turning the corner that led back to the stairs, we saw something scurry by in front of us. We jumped, frightened by the unwelcome movement.

"Rats," I said. "Oh, my God, rats."

My father, of course, would say they're mice, but I was with my mother now. Her word was the law. And to her they were rats.

My mother raised the flashlight. And we saw some more rats scurrying by.

"Mice," she said, visibly relieved. "They're only mice."

"How do you know?" I asked.

"I've always known."

12
The Princess

The synagogue was stuffed—not just with the normal Saturday morning crowd, but with our guests, too. My mother had had four days to prepare for the event, and she rose magnificently to the challenge. What a turnout! Uncle Bruce and Aunt Debbie flew in from New York on a last-minute super-saver flight. Oma Anneliese and Opa Hans-Otto made the trip in from Hanover with Tante Klara and Onkel Reinhard, my cousins Fabian and Luise, and a rented minivan. Frau Goldfarb and Frau Lewi came with some friends from the Golden Residence for the Aged. Pia and her parents, Anton, and even Yvonne were there, not to forget my Hebrew school class, including my teacher Wladimir Kasarow and my classmate Agness, whose mother turned out to be my mother's manicurist.

Even Astro*Fritz Friedrichsen made it. Imagine: they had all come to hear me read in Hebrew from the Torah, to be a part of my coming of age, to watch my mother cry when I said, "Today I am a woman." (My father cried, too.) I was impressed.

I stood up on the *bimah,* at the front of the synagogue, in a simple pantsuit, and recited in Hebrew from Genesis. I got goose bumps when I read, " 'A wind from God swept over the face of the waters. Then God said, "Let there be light." And there was light.' "

Most of the people in the congregation didn't understand a word of Hebrew, but I still like to think that they felt the emotion anyway.

Risa's spirit seemed to accompany me throughout the ceremony, especially when I stood up to give my speech. I wrote it the night before, gazing out at the stars through my window. The congregation was very still. I spoke slowly and clearly. I wanted to make sure everyone heard me, understood me, especially Risa, just in case she was out there somewhere listening in.

"I think it's very fitting that my bat mitzvah falls on the day that the story of the Creation is read from the Torah," I began. "I hope one day to be a cosmologist and understand the mysteries of the universe and its creation. Ever since I was a little girl and began looking at the stars with a telescope, I've tried to understand *how* it all began, *how* the Earth and the stars, our cosmos, was created. I asked: *What* exactly is our universe? *What* had to happen to create all this? *What* are the laws that govern our planet and universe? I looked through my telescope and tried to find answers.

"It took me a while, but eventually I realized that there is also *another* question—and you don't need a telescope to answer it. And that question is: *Why? Why* did this happen? *Why* do we exist? *Why* was our universe created? The why questions are not only harder to answer. They're also harder to ask, at least for someone like me, someone who craves facts, evidence, proof. They're harder because they touch on philosophy and poetry; they touch on matters of the heart and the spirit, not the brain.

"I know now that the Torah, that Genesis, does not mean to give us an answer as to *how* the world was created—although it may seem so. But no, God was not a professor of science." (The audience laughed here.) "No, God's in another business. Genesis is meant to express our sense of wonder, our sense of wonder at how life began. And if we learn to cherish that wonder, to keep that wonder in our hearts, allow it to lift us, to make us fly, we may, in fact, someday reach the stars, and finally understand *why*."

When I was finished, I turned to my mother and father. They were sitting next to each other, holding hands. Holding hands? My heart sang out! Was it possible? Had I brought about a reconciliation? I looked again, and saw that I was grossly mistaken. Their hands were nowhere even near each other.

For a moment I felt utterly lost and abandoned, and I'm sure I would've cried if it weren't for Rabbi Weissenberger, who cleared his throat to begin his speech to me, the bat mitzvah girl. I gave him my attention and willed myself to let go of my grief.

"For a long time," he began, "Nelly questioned the relevance of a bat mitzvah. She's what we like to call a God wrestler. And it's good that she is so. For what would the Jewish people be without their doubters? No other religion in the world encourages its people to question both God and the meaning of religion itself as Judaism does. We love skeptics. And today's bat mitzvah girl is a great one, a great skeptic in a long line of skeptics: Abraham, Moses, Job, Jacob, and Nelly Sue Edelmeister."

Everyone laughed there.

"And so," the rabbi went on, trying to control his own mirth, "I am pleased today to greet Nelly Sue Edelmeister into our community. Mazel tov!"

And a wave of *mazel tov*s arose from the congregation and, well, there I was, a woman at last.

That evening, before the party, I stood in front of my mirror and barely recognized myself in my royal-blue, off-the-shoulder, velvet gown. I had taken my glasses off (no, that's not the reason why I didn't recognize myself—I can see enough without them), and the effect was quite fetching. Behind me, in the mirror, I caught a glimpse of Prince William peeking out from my closet. I went to the closet, opened the door as wide as I could, got my footstool, and stood up next to the prince. I looked again in the mirror. If I tried hard, I could almost imagine that William and I were a flesh-and-blood couple about to go off to a ball, about to step into a horse-driven carriage. I saw the subjects of the British Empire in front of me, thousands and thousands of them, waving at us behind the police barricades. I flapped my hand in the air at them like I was Princess Diana or the Queen Mum, and—*uff!*—I fell off the stool.

I was lucky. I didn't break my arm or rip my dress. I turned to William.

"It's all your fault!" I said.

William just stared back, said nothing, did nothing, felt nothing.

I looked at the poster for a minute or two, beheld my prince in his three-piece, dark blue, pinstriped, cashmere-blend suit, his light blue shirt, his ruby red silk tie and ruby red silk kerchief, his azure blue eyes.

And then I bent down and undid the tape at the bottom of the poster, got back on the stool, stretched up a bit, and untaped the poster on top. It fell to the floor. I flattened it out as best I could, folded it up carefully, and put it on the bottom of my closet under my old Barbie doll travel case. I turned back to my mirror, smiled, and curtsied. My braid flopped over my shoulder and tickled my chest. I stood up and waved. "Hello out there!" I said, "Hi! It's me, Nelly Sue Edelmeister."

245

*　　*　　*

My mother was quite a creative makeup artist. When she was finished with me, I *really* didn't recognize myself. My God, I actually looked almost *pretty*.

I couldn't stop staring at myself in the mirror. Prettiness was an odd state of mind for me. But as foreign as it was to me, there was something about my face that looked strangely familiar. It took a moment or two for me to figure it out, but eventually I did.

I turned to my mother. "You know what? I look like you," I said.

She nodded, a little choked up; then, "Ready?"

"Almost," I said, turning back to the mirror and opening up my braid. I let my hair fall loose around my shoulders. I'd been expecting pure frizz, but what I found was mostly just curly hair. Sure, it was a little frizzy, but hey, it was all *mine*.

"Risa would be so happy to see you," my mother said, spreading my hair across my shoulders like a lustrous cape.

"I love you, Mom," I said, hugging her.

"I have something for you." She reached into her pocket and pulled out Risa's glass stone. To my astonishment, she put it around my neck and closed the clasp. "I love you, too, honeybunch," she said, kissing the top of my head.

The stone felt cool on my chest, but within seconds it seemed to take in my warmth. I watched it shimmer in the light.

"Risa told me to let you wear it when you figured

out how to make light shine in the dark places of your life," my mother said. "And you did."

There were enough *kasha varnishkes* at Minsky's to feed the czar's army. Everything was there: food and wine, flowers, music, the court photographer, and lots and lots of guests. Everyone came. It felt like the whole synagogue was there: my parents' friends, my friends, my relatives, everyone. Everyone, that is, except one person. Maximilian Minsky.

My eyes searched the crowd, darting here and there past dozens and dozens of familiar and unfamiliar faces. I walked through the throngs, shaking hands, accepting congratulations, *mazel tov*s, and letting everyone kiss me, and pinch me, and hug me to death. And through it all I looked and looked. But no Max.

My father guided me to the center of the floor to dance. He twirled me around and around, the proud bat mitzvah father. In fast motion I saw my aunt Debbie and uncle Bruce waltzing, Frau and Herr Pankewitz, Astro*Fritz Friedrichsen and Frau Goldfarb, Rabbi Weissenberger and his wife, my grandparents, and not to believe: Anton and Pia were dancing together, too!

My eyes made out Melissa Minsky, in white, not far from me, moving among her guests like a queen, gracious and ever beautiful. On the other side of the restaurant was my mother, in black, the fast talker, one tough cookie. They were like two generals setting up enemy camps. My father and I were caught in a no man's land between them—and the battle hadn't even yet begun.

So on and on we danced, my father and I, my eyes traveling through the crowd, searching, searching ... until, at last, in the distance, a figure began to take shape. Was I dreaming? Was it possible? Was *that* Max?

Standing across the room was a tall young man in a three-piece, dark blue, pinstriped, cashmere-blend suit, a light blue shirt, a ruby red silk tie, and a ruby red silk kerchief in his breast pocket.

I raised my hand to my chest to steady myself. My fingers grazed Risa's glass stone and I felt its warmth, which was the warmth of my own body, and saw it glitter, which was the excitement in my heart.

The dense sea of faces and bodies before me seemed to part. My father drifted off to the side, the music softened, I could hear my heart beat. And suddenly Max and I were alone on the floor, alone in the world, in the universe, slowly, ever so slowly, gravitating toward each other. And as we came together, as Max lowered his face toward mine, as I died a thousand deaths waiting to feel the first warmth of his lips, he simply whispered softly in my ear, "It itches. The damn suit itches. I'm allergic to cashmere."

But then, despite his discomfort, he smiled and took my hand to lead me across the floor to dance. And as he drew me toward him and held me tight, I think I understood for the first time in my life what it felt like to be a princess.

But I wasn't, of course. I was just me, Nelly Sue Edelmeister, thirteen years old, future cosmologist, once known as Nerd Nelly, now known as Nelly van Exelmeister; me, daughter of Lucy Bloom-Edelmeister, the belle of the ball, and Bernhard Nicholas Edelmeister, aka Bazooka Benny, the Prince of Deception; me, Nelly, Pia's vice and Max's first; me, Nelly Sue Edelmeister, beneficiary of Risa Ginsberg, no longer among us and sorely missed.

But before I get into any more details, I think I better stop here. I can already hear my mother complaining. "Enough is enough," she's saying. "Too much epilogue is too much epilogue. Get out of the story. Shut down the press."

Maybe this once I'll take her advice. I mean, I only wanted to tell you all about me and Prince William. And I did. Right?

GLOSSARY

bat mitzvah (Hebrew) coming-of-age ceremony for girls, similar to the bar mitzvah for boys, in which adolescents take their place as adults in the eyes of the Jewish community.

bimah (Hebrew) the elevated platform in the synagogue on which the Torah is read

bubeleh (Yiddish) literally, "little grandma"; a term of endearment, like *darling,* used for both girls and boys

chutzpah (Yiddish) nerve, daring

currywurst a fast food developed in Berlin that consists of sliced bratwurst smothered in tomato sauce and sprinkled with curry powder and paprika

Doppelkopf (German) a four-player card game, similar to bridge in its use of a trump suit

Ess a bissel (Yiddish) "Eat a little." Depending on the mother or grandmother saying this, "a little" could encompass a wide range of calories!

haftarah or **Haftorah** (Hebrew) a chapter of the Prophets, read in the synagogue after the weekly Torah portion; each portion of the Torah has a specific corresponding haftarah. At his or her bar or bat mitzvah, a young person chants the haftarah for that Sabbath.

hidur penei zakein (Hebrew) to honor the elderly, which is a mitzvah, or good deed

Kaddish (Hebrew, from the Aramaic *kadosh,* meaning "holy") a prayer praising God, recited after a Bible reading; has become known as the Mourner's Prayer

kasha varnishkes (Yiddish) an eastern European dish made from kasha (buckwheat groats) and bow-tie noodles, sautéed with onions in chicken fat and butter. This is not only Nelly's favorite dish but also the author's.

kibbud av va'em (Hebrew) honoring one's father and mother—a Biblical commandment

Kindchen (German) an endearment meaning "little child," akin to "sweetie"

klezmer (Yiddish, from the Hebrew, *klei-zemer*, meaning "musical instruments") traditionally, a small band of Jewish folk musicians whose style was once typical of small villages in eastern Europe, now popular in new forms. The group often includes a clarinet and could be called a form of Jewish jazz.

mark German monetary unit at the time of the story

mazel tov (Hebrew) "Congratulations!" So mazel tov! if you've gotten this far in this glossary!

Midrash (Hebrew) a collection of commentaries on the Torah

oy gevalt (Yiddish) "good heavens!" This all-purpose exclamation can express anything from extreme pain to extreme happiness, and everything in between.

Parshas Bereishis (Hebrew) *Parshas* means the weekly Torah portion; Bereishis is the very beginning of the first of the five Books of Moses. So in this case, the Torah portion is from Bereishis. An older person from eastern

Europe or Germany would use the Ashkenazic pronunciation: *Parshas Bereishis,* whereas the final *s* in each word would be pronounced as a *t* (for the Hebrew letter *tav*) by Sephardic Jews or in modern Hebrew.

Riefenstahl, Leni infamous German filmmaker whose movie *Triumph of the Will* showed the Nazis in a positive light. She lived a very long life and died at the age of 101.

Schätzchen (German) literally, "little treasure"—an endearment

schlep (Yiddish) to carry, lug, or to move from one point to another as if one were trapped in molasses. Also used to refer to sloppy or ragged-looking individuals (perhaps because they look like something the cat dragged in). Such a person can be called a schlepper.

schmaltz (Yiddish) melted chicken fat, used in cooking; also means something that is overly sentimental, such as a movie, book, or greeting card that tries much too hard to touch your feelings

shayne maidele (Yiddish) beautiful girl

shivah (Hebrew) the seven days of mourning for the dead, beginning immediately after the funeral

Shoah (Hebrew) literally, "the burning"; the Holocaust

shofar (Hebrew) a ram's horn, blown in the synagogue on Rosh Hashanah and Yom Kippur. It is a reminder of the ram that God allowed Abraham to sacrifice in place of Isaac.

shul (Yiddish) synagogue

Tillim (Hebrew) the Psalms

tochis (Yiddish) derrière; Americanized as *tush*

Torah (Hebrew) the Pentateuch, or Five Books of Moses: Genesis, Exodus, Leviticus, Numbers, and Deuteronomy

Thanks …

to all the people who read this book when it was a work in progress and helped shape it with their encouragement, enthusiasm, and criticism: Esmé Barcomi, Nina Bernstein, Atina Grossmann, Jason Honig, Tina Kemnitz, Rachel Libeskind, Joachim Pietzsch, Alan Posener, Antje von Stemm, Anke Sterneborg;

to everyone who let me pick their brains: Chiara Czernobilsky, Daphne Czernobilsky, Dietmar Fuerst from the Archenhold Planetarium, Wendy Kloke, Shelley Kupferberg, Dr. Ingrid Kutzner, Cornelia Martyn, Rabbi Walter Rothschild;

to Nelly and Max Mecklenburg, brother and sister team, for letting me use their names;

to Susanne Koppe for being just about the world's greatest editor, and I'm not kidding;

to Susan Stan for believing that this book should not just be read by Europeans—and

to Marc Aronson for making it happen;

to my husband, Eberhard Delius, without whom I could never have written this book;

to my son, Noah Delius, without whom I would never have understood why I wrote it.